Metafictions?

Reflexivity in Contemporary Texts

Wenche Ommundsen

MELBOURNE UNIVERSITY PRESS

1993

First published 1993
Designed by text-art
Typeset in 10½ point Garamond
Printed in Malaysia by
SRM Production Services Shd Bhd for
Melbourne University Press, Carlton, Victoria 3053
U.S.A. and Canada: International Specialized Book Services, Inc.,
5804 N.E. Hassalo Street, Portland, Oregon 97213-3644
United Kingdom and Europe: University College London Press,
Gower Street, London WC1E 6BT, U.K.

© Wenche Ommundsen 1993

ISSN 1039-6128

National Library of Australia Cataloguing-in-Publication data

Ommundsen, Wenche.
   Metafictions?
   Bibliography.
   Includes index.
   ISBN 0 522 84524 X.
   1. Fiction–20th century–History and criticism. 2. Fiction–
Technique. 3. Experimental fiction–History and criticism. I. Title.
(Series: Interpretations).
801.953

Metafictions?

Interpretations

This series provides clearly written and up-to-date introductions to recent theories and critical practices in the humanities and social sciences.

General Editors
Stephen Knight (De Montfort University)
and Ken Ruthven (University of Melbourne)

Advisory Board
Tony Bennett (Griffith University)
Penny Boumelha (University of Adelaide)
John Frow (University of Queensland)
Sneja Gunew (University of Victoria, British Columbia)
Robert Hodge (Murdoch University)
Terry Threadgold (Monash University)

Already published:
Cultural Materialism, by Andrew Milner
Nuclear Criticism, by Ken Ruthven

In preparation:
Foucauldian criticism, by Alec McHoul and Wendy Grace
Framing and interpretation, by Gale MacLachlan and Ian Reid
Aboriginality, by Tim Rowse
Postmodern socialism, by Peter Beilharz
Multicultural literature studies, edited by Sneja Gunew
Post-colonial literary studies, by Anne Brewster

Contents

Preface

In the early 1970s, when I was studying 'French as a Foreign Language' at the University of Lausanne, in Switzerland, I occasionally ventured into the lecture theatres where 'real' French was taught to the natives. Here I discovered something called the *nouveau roman*, and, at about the same time, witnessed an amazing performance by a couple of visiting Frenchmen who were doing unspeakable things to Baudelaire's 'Cats'. What they were doing, I later found out, was called structuralism. The excitement which surrounded the new novel and the newest criticism and theory in those days was contagious, and it was with some missionary zeal that I carried it with me into English studies, which by comparison seemed rather stuffy and old-fashioned. I soon found that I was not the only one to do so; in fact, it seemed that just about everybody had made the same discoveries, and that the whole world of 'English literature' was being refashioned according to French writing—and writing about writing. Today, twenty years later, I often wonder why we all seemed to have the same ideas at about the same time, and why we continued, for quite a while, to think of ourselves as pioneers when the field we were charting was more thoroughly explored than any before it in the history of literary studies. As the dust settles on the structuralist and post-structuralist 'revolution' I have become more interested in connections than in newness: connections between the new novel (or the postmodern novel) and older fictional forms, connections between current literary theory and earlier ideas about the nature of literary texts, connections, finally, between literary theory and literary practice. Metafiction, which exists at the intersection between theory and fiction, enables me to explore a number of such connections at the same time as it allows me to indulge in a bit of personal nostalgia. Even today, a good metafiction will send a tingle down my spine which forever will be connected to the shock which, as we perceived it, shook the very foundations of the venerable *Ancienne Académie* and reinvented literature right in front of our—oh, so naive—eyes.

My journey through words and worlds has left behind a trail of debt stretching from Norway through Switzerland, the US and Britain to Australia, a debt so extensive that it cannot possibly be acknowledged in detail here. To all those teachers, fellow students and colleagues—hail—and would that our journeys, both intellectual and physical, intersect again some time. My present and former colleagues at Deakin University have helped and inspired me in various ways, and I should like to thank in particular Ian Reid, for fostering my interest in narrative theory, and Sneja Gunew, for her gentle reminders that all genres and canons can—and must—be challenged.

I am grateful to Deakin University for granting me study leave and teaching release, and to Saint David's University College, University of Wales, for a Visiting Research Fellowship during which much of the research for this book was carried out. Earlier versions of my ideas on metafiction have been published in *AUMLA* and *Southern Review*, and I am grateful to the editors of those journals for permission to reproduce them here. Figures 1 and 2 are adapted from M. Boyd, *The Reflexive Novel*, Figure 3 from R. Siegle, *The Politics of Reflexivity*. Figure 4 is reproduced by kind permission of Madame Magritte, Paris, and the Los Angeles County Museum of Art.

Marian Boreland provided competent research assistance for the completion of the manuscript and Kay Perry offered invaluable advice on language matters that had eluded my not perfectly anglicised tongue.

My family has been a source of both help and hindrance, while the effect of this book, for them, has been unambiguous: a major nuisance. Now that it is all over I wish to thank David for hours of listening (or pretending to listen) to my arguments and anxieties, and Camilla and Emma, for providing a healthy, if not always favourable, perspective on my metafictions.

Wenche Ommundsen, January 1993

Definitions

A self-conscious novel, briefly, is a novel that systematically flaunts its own condition of artifice and that by so doing probes into the problematic relationship between real-seeming artifice and reality.

Robert Alter

This intense self-reflexiveness of metafiction is caused by the fact that the only certain reality for the metafictionist is the reality of his own discourse; thus, his fiction turns in upon itself, transforming the process of writing into the subject of writing.

Mas'ud Zavarzadeh

'Metafiction,' as it has now been named, is fiction about fiction—that is, fiction that includes within itself a commentary on its own narrative and/ or linguistic identity.

Linda Hutcheon

Metafiction refers to other fictions, not to worlds outside or beyond, not to 'reality.'

Hans Skei

In providing a critique of their own methods of construction, such writings not only examine the fundamental structures of narrative fiction, they also explore the possible fictionality of the world outside the literary fictional text.

Patricia Waugh

Metafictions—fictions which examine fictional systems, how they are created, and the way in which reality is transformed by and filtered through narrative assumptions and conventions.

Larry McCaffery

Because they do not seek to tell yet another story but to examine the story-telling process itself, reflexive novels must be seen as works of literary theory and criticism.

Michael Boyd

In the final analysis reflexivity is a way of understanding the semiotic, philosophical, and ideological processes taking place in any narrative alongside those issues our existing poetics equips us to find.

Robert Siegle

1

Introductions

Serious modern fiction has only one subject: the difficulty of writing serious modern fiction. First, it has fully accepted that it is only fiction, can only be fiction, will never be anything but fiction, and therefore has no business at all tampering with real life or reality . . .

Second. The natural consequence of this is that writing *about* fiction has become a far more important matter than writing fiction itself. It's one of the best ways you can tell the true novelist nowadays. He's not going to waste his time over the messy garage-mechanic drudge of assembling stories and characters on paper. (Fowles, 1982:117–18)

This passage from John Fowles's novel *Mantissa* does *not* offer a very useful description of 'serious modern fiction'. It does not even give a good definition of metafiction, or reflexive fiction (the kind of fiction which *does* take fiction-writing as its subject matter). What it does, however, is point to a number of questions and controversies which have been associated with metafiction in recent critical debates and which it is the aim of this book to explore. What exactly is the nature of 'metafiction' and 'reflexivity' and what is their place in contemporary fiction? Is metafiction a sub-genre of the novel, or is it a tendency inherent in *all* fiction? What sort of relationship, if any, can exist between metafiction and the world outside the fictional universe? And finally, as Patricia Waugh (1984:7) so pointedly asks, 'Why are they saying such awful things about it?'.

Mantissa is best characterised as a parody of metafiction. In a grey room with soft, padded walls one male and one female protagonist engage in seemingly endless variations of sexual intercourse, interspersed with (mostly hostile) verbal exchange and the odd rest period. The implications of their acts are soon revealed: the man, Miles Green, is an author; the woman, Erato, is his muse; the padded room is the inside of the author's brain and their intercourse a metaphor for the act of fictional creation (together they 'give birth' to the story in which they figure). Erato, muse of love-poetry and fiction transported straight from ancient Greek mythology is, of course, a rather anachronistic presence in a modern novel, but it is her ignorance of the latest fashions in fiction and criticism which enables Miles to deliver his lecture on the nature of serious modern fiction, and, incidentally, to show his own superiority over the naive conception of literature inherited from the ancients which still, it would seem, holds sway in many circles today. The trouble is, of course, that it is not the muse and her outdated ideas that are being mocked here, but the serious modern author himself: the main target for Fowles's irony is precisely the kind of fiction which (like *Mantissa*) turns its back on the real world to indulge in claustrophobic introspection. Miles Green, who insists that the sex *he* writes about is 'absolutely clinical . . . rather cleverly deprived of all eroticism' (Fowles, 1982:119) and who scorns as boring and irrelevant the things women and men are up to when they are not figuring as metaphors for important literary functions, thus stands as a kind of anti-model, representing the worst tendencies in contemporary metafiction. Ridiculing his pretentious theorising and hinting that the 'clinical' sex in his fiction in fact disguises cheap and sexist pornography, *Mantissa*, it would seem, in the end affirms the value of writing dealing with real people, real problems and the real world. Writing, in other words, which is everything *Mantissa* itself is not.

Against Miles Green's vision of a literature blissfully free from the 'garage-mechanic drudge' of stories, characters and reality stands the view that metafiction through introspection betrays the true mission of fiction, that of reflecting and commenting on the extra-textual world. But underlying *both* of these seemingly opposing views lies an assumption which has been common to much writing on metafiction in the last decades: fiction cannot, at the same time, be about itself and about something else. Exposing its own artefact, admitting that it is a linguistic and narrative construct and not a reflection of real things, metafiction has forfeited its right to interact in any meaningful way with the world. Deeming its self-absorption irresponsible and morally reprehensible, many critics have called for a return to more socially responsive modes of writing. Robert Scholes, for example, writes in *Fabulation and Metafiction*:

> It is now time for man to turn civilization in the direction of integration and away from alienation, to bring human life back into harmony with the universe.
>
> For fiction, self-reflection is a narcissistic way of avoiding this great task. It produces a certain kind of pleasure, no doubt, this masturbatory reveling in self-scrutiny; but it also generates great feelings of guilt—not because what it is doing is bad, but because of what it is avoiding. (Scholes, 1979:217–18)

Reading contemporary metafiction rather than the criticism it has inspired, one is less likely, however, to conclude that such writing deals with masturbatory self-scrutiny to the exclusion of any involvement with reality or history. The case of Salman Rushdie provides an outstanding (and terrifying) example of how politics, religion and (meta)fiction interact: if it had been true that the exploration of fictional systems prevents involvement with extra-textual realities, his writing would have been unlikely to provoke violent reactions; it did, in fact, result in a death sentence against the author. The stories, lies and conventions of metafiction have equivalents in the real world. Luisa Valenzuela's *The Lizard's Tail* rewrites the history of Argentina in overtly fictional terms, showing, however, that politics is the supreme maker of fictions. Peter Carey's *Illywhacker* and Murray Bail's *Holden's Performance* explore the relationship between the (acknowledged) lies of fiction and the (unacknowledged) fictions which constitute the myths and histories of the Australian national identity. Even when the 'world' of a literary text is demonstrably unreal, as is the case with the brain/

room of *Mantissa*, it does not preclude interaction with stories that circulate in the real world. Margaret Atwood's *The Handmaid's Tale* is set in a dystopic future society, further distanced from the reader by the framing fiction of an even more remote future examining the main narrative as a questionable historical document; its overtly fictitious world nevertheless offers today's reader a highly pertinent analysis of gendered politics in our own society. *Mantissa* itself, through the textual as well as sexual intercourses between Miles and Erato, rehearses a great many historically relevant myths of sex and gender in addition to those concerning the roles of readers and writers.

One of the aims of the present book is precisely to challenge the perceived incompatibility between reflexivity and involvement with reality. I will not be the first to do so. A number of commentators on metafiction (see Waugh, 1984; Hutcheon, 1988, 1989; Siegle, 1986) have in recent years drawn on the teaching of structuralist and post-structuralist literary theory to point to similarities between the ways in which factual and fictional discourses construct the world. 'If our knowledge of this world is now seen to be mediated through language, then literary fiction (worlds constructed entirely of language) becomes a useful model for learning about the construction of "reality" itself', writes Patricia Waugh (1984:3). Metafiction, considered from such a perspective, becomes not so much divorced from reality as centrally concerned with the ways in which the real is produced and mediated. Throughout this book it will be argued that the perceived and to my view misleading opposition between reflexivity and reality, or between metafiction and realism, may have come about through the construction of metafiction itself as a genre or category seemingly distinct from 'ordinary' fiction. Reflexivity, I will suggest, is best understood as a dimension present in all literary texts and central to all literary analysis; a function which by analysing literary processes enables us to understand the processes by which we read the world as text.

Reading *Mantissa* one is faced with a problem inherent in many double-coded texts: that of knowing whether to produce a 'straight' interpretation of the textual indicators or to read them through the distorting lens of irony. Metafiction relies centrally on textual strategies such as metaphor, irony and parody, all of which require

4

the reader to recognise more than one level of meaning. *Mantissa* provides an outstanding example of this. I have already suggested that Miles Green's lecture on serious modern fiction should be read against the grain, as a mockery rather than a celebration of fictional self-referentiality. But the case is more complicated still. It turns out that the alternative views on modern fiction presented by Erato in her numerous guises fare no better: the muse's naive belief that fiction should simply reflect life and her various politicised versions of art (feminist, pseudo-Marxist) are similarly ridiculed. It also becomes clear that Miles, for all his limitations, nevertheless *is* a persona for the author, John Fowles himself: the novel contains numerous references to Fowles's earlier books (*The Collector, The Magus, The French Lieutenant's Woman*), with suggestions that these are precisely the self-obsessed artefacts which are being mocked here. Or are they? It is also possible, I think, to read *Mantissa* as a criticism, not of contemporary fiction, but of the way this fiction has been read by literary criticism. It is criticism, particularly academic criticism, which has categorised Fowles's work as metafiction, arguing that it is more concerned with 'the difficulty of writing serious modern fiction' than with stories and characters. It is the critics, not Fowles, who claim that a text which displays an awareness of the fiction-making process cannot at the same time be concerned with matters outside the fictional universe. According to such a reading, then, Miles Green and his monstrous fictions do not represent the 'real' John Fowles at all, but are the products of wilful critical distortion.

The problem for the reader is that no one reading of *Mantissa* can ever be produced as final. The web of irony is so complex that double coding turns into multiple coding and it becomes difficult for either reader or text to exert any real control over meaning. It is this kind of undecidability which has earned contemporary metafiction much of its hostile criticism. Charles Newman writes: 'Irony is no longer a dynamic principle, but the inert substance of the matter. One becomes ironic about irony—infinite reduction becomes the engine of narrative momentum' (1985:54). But against Newman it is possible to argue that metafiction's playful juggling of textual meaning points to the way meaning is produced outside fiction: 'truth' may be as variable, as historically and culturally

contingent as our textual interpretations, and the reader's awareness of this should make for critical engagement with texts and
truths, not for inertia.

The complex 'case' of *Mantissa* need not, perhaps, be read as an
indictment of reflexivity in contemporary fiction. By presenting
itself as a parody, an extreme and distorted version of metafictional
self-obsession, the novel points to fictions in which the reflexive
element functions to enrich the reader's interaction with stories and
realities. It is the phenomenon of reflexivity itself which is finally
held up for scrutiny: its implications for the reading of fictional texts,
its critical uses and abuses.

Metafiction: modes, methods and meanings

'You are about to begin reading Italo Calvino's new novel, *If on a
winter's night a traveler.*' This is the first sentence of Calvino's book
by that name, already signalling a number of metafictional concerns: a reminder that this story is a *novel*, the function of the author
and the fact of publication, the role of the reader in the fictional
experience. By means of an intrusive narrator addressing the reader
directly, Calvino clearly labels his novel as a metafiction; the reader
is from the very start alerted to the fact that this will be a book about
reading, writing and fictionality.

I am not, however, quoting from Calvino's novel here. The novel
I have in front of me starts like this:

> You are about to begin reading Italo Calvino's new novel, *If on
> a winter's night a traveler.* These are the words Italo Calvino
> selected to open his novel *If on a winter's night a traveller.*
> Astonishingly he sets them out in the same order. (Henshaw,
> 1988:3)

This opening is taken from *Out of the Line of Fire*, a novel by the
Australian writer Mark Henshaw. By choosing to quote Calvino,
Henshaw obviously echoes the metafictional concerns signalled by
the original first sentence, but he does other things as well. The use
of an intertextual reference, another device frequently employed in
metafiction, enables Henshaw to introduce other preoccupations
central to *his* book. The reference to Calvino identifies *Out of the*

Line of Fire as a book about other books: Henshaw's narrator, himself a writer, will throughout his story quote from and discuss other texts and other writers. The quotation also speaks of a certain playfulness. After all, Calvino's first sentence, addressed to Henshaw's reader, is simply incorrect: she or he is about to read an altogether different book. This opening, moreover, allows Henshaw's narrator to raise a matter which will be of major importance to him: the question of translation. He notes that the word 'traveller' is spelt in the British manner, with a double l, in the title, but with a single l, according to American usage, in the first sentence, and remarks that Calvino's novel of course doesn't start like this at all; *its* first sentence is in Italian. 'And doesn't this alert us', he asks,

> to the fact that, as a translation, it has been filtered through a particular linguistic, cultural and conceptual sieve, that an English translation is likely to be substantially different from an American one, and that if we were to compare the cumulative effect of the differences which might arise in these two hypothetical translations against the original, might we not end up reading three entirely different novels? (ibid.:3–4)

Finally, the beginning of Calvino's novel allows Henshaw's narrator to speculate on the beginning of novels in general, the difficulty of beginning and the need to 'ensnare the reader, to capture his or her attention'.

My own reason for using Calvino and Henshaw's sentence to start this section (apart from the wish to ensnare *my* reader) is that it offers a compact illustration of the wide and complex spectrum of metafictional methods and metafictional concerns. Direct reader address and intertextual allusion are only two of the many techniques reflexive texts deploy, sometimes singly, sometimes together, sometimes even, as in Henshaw's opening lines, simultaneously. The *meanings* of the metafictional enquiry are, as this example suggests, equally numerous, ranging from speculations about the functioning of the literary artefact to investigations into the nature of all 'linguistic, cultural and conceptual sieves'.

The ostentatious, intrusive narrator or author-figure, interrupting the story to air his or her preoccupations with the processes of fiction-writing, is perhaps the most explicit way of expressing a reflexive awareness. The intrusion may be of a purely personal, confessional nature, referring to the act of writing or to the writer's 'real' life. Examples of this are Gerald Murnane's 'I dislike what I have just written. I believe my editor too will dislike it when she reads it. I had not meant to compose that sort of sentence when I began to write' (1988:2), and David Lodge's 'I teach English literature at a redbrick university and write novels in my spare time, slowly, and hustled by history' (1980:243). Elsewhere, the intrusion may deal in a more theoretical way with the nature of fiction, or even, as in this example from A. S. Byatt's *Possession*, the nature of metafiction:

> And it is probable that there is an element of superstitious dread in any self-referring, self-reflexive, inturned postmodernist mirror-game or plot-coil that recognises that it has got out of hand, that connections proliferate apparently at random, that is to say, with equal verisimilitude, apparently in response to some ferocious ordering principle, not controlled by conscious intention, which would of course, being a good postmodernist intention, *require* the aleatory or the multivalent or the 'free', but structuring, but controlling, but driving, to some—to what?—end. (Byatt, 1990:421–2)

Interrupting the narrative flow to digress about the life and thoughts of the author, or to theorise about literature, may give the impression that the real world has intruded into the fictional universe. But 'reality' in metafiction is always a highly suspect concept. The real itself becomes fictionalised, becomes, instead, a narrative level, or 'diegetic level', as it is sometimes called in narrative theory. A favourite ploy in metafiction consists in transgressing diegetic levels so that the inhabitants of one fictional world (for example that of the author) start interacting with those of another (the characters of the author's fiction). In Flann O'Brien's novel *At Swim-Two-Birds* the (fictional) author Dermot Trellis sexually assaults his own character Sheila Lamont and has a son, Orlick, by her. Later, in a fiction written by Orlick, Trellis is judged by a jury consisting of his own characters, found guilty of severe mistreatment and punished.

The violation of narrative levels—variously referred to as 'metalepsis', 'tangled hierarchies' or 'strange loops' (see Genette,

1980; McHale, 1987; Hofstadter, 1980)—works to destabilise the fictional illusion, calling attention to its fabricated nature. Reading about a character hearing the ticking of a typewriter writing the story in which she figures (in Muriel Spark's *The Comforters*), or about a reader getting involved in the life of characters she reads about (in Elizabeth Jolley's *Miss Peabody's Inheritance*), does not exactly *destroy* the fictional illusion (after all, we knew all along the story was a fiction); it does, however, force us to reflect on the nature of that illusion, and our own complicity in its creation.

Structural incoherence of many kinds is common in metafiction. A text may refuse to comply with expectations set up by the genre to which it belongs: the coherence of fictional characters, for example, or the idea of a single ending. It may also transgress generic boundaries, including within a work of fiction elements normally found in other types of writing. The presence of footnotes generally points to genres such as criticism, historiography or other kinds of scholarly writing; when they occur in a work of fiction, they upset our generic expectations, forcing a reconsideration of how texts are sorted into categories, and how the category itself determines our mode of reception. Incoherence may occur at the level of the individual word or sentence, also with the general effect of making the reader stop and reconsider reading and sense-making practices which are taken for granted, thought of as 'natural'. By intensifying the artefact, making the transition from text to meaning more complex, reflexive fiction thus calls attention to the material existence of language and fictional systems, the 'stuff' of literature which the reader otherwise tends to overlook.

Metafictional awareness is not always as explicitly or unambiguously stated as in *Mantissa*, or in the other examples cited here. Frequently, an element in the text will serve a double function, and it is up to the reader to determine whether to read such an element reflexively or not. Intertextual allusions are not always detected, and even if they are, they are not necessarily read reflexively in the sense that they refer to the literary experience as such. Many novels about artists and writers may or may not be read as metafictions: it is possible to read *A Portrait of the Artist as a Young Man* as being about Joyce as an artist and the genesis of *A Portrait* . . . itself, but many readers (and critics) have interpreted Stephen Dedalus and his artistic aspirations differently.

In order to read a textual element, such as Stephen Dedalus, as part of a metafictional enquiry, the reader needs to recognise a double function, or a metaphorical relationship, at work in the text: the element is at the same time part of the story and something else (comment on the story). This kind of relationship is generally referred to as *mise en abyme*, which means an embedded self-representation or mirror-image of the text within the text. This French term, borrowed from heraldry (where it refers to a small shield depicted within a larger one), was first used in this sense by André Gide, who in his novel *The Counterfeiters* includes a fictional novelist writing a novel also entitled *The Counterfeiters*. The *mise en abyme* may, as in this case, refer to the whole work which includes it; it may also refer to a particular element within that work, or it may take as its subject the processes of fictional creation and communication. (For a detailed discussion of types of *mises en abyme* see Dällenbach, 1989.) Thus Lily Briscoe's painting, in Virginia Woolf's *To the Lighthouse*, may be read as representing the novel in which it figures: its efforts to capture the essence of Mrs Ramsay, its final vision. In David Lodge's novel *How Far Can You Go?* the Catholic faith is made to parallel the mimetic illusion in fiction, and in Balzac's 'Sarrasine', as read by Roland Barthes, the embedded story-telling scene prefigures the impact of 'Sarrasine' itself on its readers. Related to the *mise en abyme* is the plot allegory, also depending for its metafictional realisation on the reader's awareness of double (or multiple) levels of interpretation. Typical plot allegories in metafiction include the sexual act, figuring, as in *Mantissa*, the act of fictional creation, and the detective, who in several novels by Marguerite Duras and Alain Robbe-Grillet, for example, functions as a model for the reader's activity. Game structures, another model for plot allegory, are frequently linked to the codes of fictional systems, combining determined patterns with elements of chance. A recent novel by Finola Moorhead, entitled *Still Murder*, combines the function of the detective with the image of the jigsaw puzzle to symbolise the reader's quest for meaning.

Parody is a particular form of intertextuality much favoured as a means of raising reflexive concerns. Imitating, but also distancing itself from its model, the parody on the one hand invites the pleasure of recognition, on the other critical reappraisal. The object of the parody may be a specific text; it may also be a fictional convention or a genre or mode of writing. Iris Murdoch's *The Black Prince* and Angela Carter's *Wise Children* take as their models plays by Shakespeare (*Hamlet* and *A Midsummer Night's Dream*, respectively), John Fowles parodies the omniscient narrator in *The French Lieutenant's Woman*. Cervantes' *Don Quixote*, often referred to as the first novel *and* the first metafiction, is a parody of the romance genre, so are a number of recent texts such as David Lodge's *Small World* and A. S. Byatt's *Possession*. Angela Carter rewrites fairy tales parodically, Nabokov parodies literary criticism in *Pale Fire*, and Malcolm Bradbury parodies post-structuralist theory in *Mensonge*. Popular forms of fiction such as detective fiction, science fiction and Mills and Boon-type romance are frequently the targets for metafictional parody, so are fictional narratives in other media: Hollywood movies, popular cartoons, television soap opera.

A number of critics writing about metafiction (see esp. Ricardou, 1975; Scholes 1979; Hutcheon, 1984) have attempted to subdivide this category according to either fictional method or thematic concern. Linda Hutcheon, in what is undoubtedly the most interesting of these typologies, distinguishes on the one hand between overt and covert (explicit and implicit) modes of metafiction, on the other between diegetic and linguistic reflexivity (situated on the level of narrative structure and the level of language, respectively). But while most readers will agree that certain texts display their reflexivity in explicit or unambiguous ways, whereas others are much less explicit, the construction of a typology based on such criteria will always be problematic. Individual techniques such as parody may be explicitly reflexive in certain texts, much less so in others, and readers may not always agree on whether a text should be put in one or the other category. More importantly, most reflexive fictions combine a number of techniques and a number of preoccupations in their metafictional apparatus, overt, covert, diegetic, linguistic. Mark Henshaw's *Out of the Line of Fire*, for example, addresses the full range of techniques and themes referred to above, sometimes in explicitly reflexive commentary, sometimes in ways which will only be read as reflexive if the reader is prepared to make the necessary connections. A typology which in the final count is more interesting for its own inner coherence than for its ability to classify and define literary texts thus fails to justify its existence.

Metafiction presents its readers with allegories of the fictional experience, calling our attention to the functioning of the fictional artefact, its creation and reception, its participation in the meaning-making systems of our culture. Fiction is in its turn allegorised, made to stand as a model for all acts of cultural construction and interpretation, for the myths and ideologies which organise our reality according to narrative structures. History, politics, gender, race, nationality, the individual, reality—all of these concepts can be read as systems of signs, cultural constructs, or texts. Our perception of human life is organised, as Lyotard has argued, according to our society's narratives of what is true, just or real (see Lyotard, 1984). Reflexive texts can thus be seen to function as microcosms, pointing to larger structures in the human world. Muriel Spark and John Fowles present omniscient author-figures, organising the novel from the position of an omnipotent god in accordance with Judaeo-Christian models of the world. In *The Magus* Fowles eventually removes the author, and his characters find themselves in a universe organised according to a different principle, an existentialist void. Other writers (Thomas Pynchon, B. S. Johnson) have produced fictions and worlds where random-ness, the lack of a controlling power, is the construction model.

This text–world connection, whether or not explicitly fore-grounded by reflexive fiction, is what makes metafiction relevant in more ways than as a substitute for literary theory. The meaning of metafiction is, ultimately, neither more nor less than the meaning of the human world.

The metafictional double-take

Presenting a critique of fiction from within a fiction, metafiction raises a logical problem common to all meta-objects: is it possible to be, at the same time, both object and comment on that object, both product and process of representation? Is Erato truly a character of fiction, or is she simply a vehicle for theorising about fiction? Are we to read Miles Green's 'lecture' as a comment on modern writing, and on *Mantissa* itself, or should we regard it merely as a function within the fictional universe of this particular novel, a way, perhaps, of identifying Miles as a character? Is it possible to read the text simultaneously in both these ways, or does that constitute a logical contradiction? As a number of critics have suggested (see Hofstadter, 1980; Rose, 1979; Daniel, 1988), we are faced here with a dilemma similar to that of the Cretan liar, who, stating 'All Cretans are liars' and 'I am Cretan' paradoxically denies the possibility of both truth and falsehood. 'Surely the analysis of water should not itself be wet', writes C.S.Lewis (quoted in Brooke-Rose, 1981:344), but it is also possible to argue that wetness is a quality that must be embraced for the phenomenon 'water' to be apprehended at all. In the case of metafiction the paradox of self-referentiality eventually turns not only on literary self-representation, but also on metafictional writing outside fictional texts. Literary criticism, which like its object of study functions through the medium of language, thus becomes implicated in its critique. What conventions, linguistic and narrative, govern the discourses of literary commentary? Can criticism ever hope to escape fictionality, to stand outside the literary processes it takes for its object of analysis? One of the important lessons of metafiction may well be that all writing about literature (not excluding this book) is forced, reflexively, to examine its own practices, to question the stories it tells about literature and the critical categories it constructs to accommodate them.

How to Recognise a Metafiction When You See One: A Short Critical History and Three Models

Discovery and definition of a genre

The term 'metafiction', according to most accounts, was coined by the American novelist and critic William H. Gass, who, describing the fiction of Jorge Luis Borges, John Barth and Flann O'Brien, writes, 'Indeed, many of the so-called antinovels are really metafictions' (Gass, 1971:25). The coinage was not particularly original: attention to 'meta-phenomena' has in the second half of this century been common in a number of disciplines (Gass himself mentions meta-theorems in mathematics and logic) and the French critic Roland Barthes (1972:97) had in the short essay 'Literature and Metalanguage', first published in 1959, identified the double consciousness of contemporary literature as both 'literature object' and 'metaliterature'. A great number of other names have been given to the same type of writing: self-conscious, reflexive (or self-reflexive), self-referential, introspective, introverted, narcissistic or auto-representational, surfiction, antifiction, fabulation, neo-baroque fiction and postmodernist fiction. These terms are not perfectly synonymous: surfiction and fabulation have sometimes been contrasted with metafiction, and postmodernism, in fiction and elsewhere, is, as we will see later, a category so complex and disputed that its relationship to metafiction cannot be precisely defined.

While some critical consensus seems to exist regarding the basic definition of metafiction or reflexive fiction (it is *about* fiction), critics vary considerably in their accounts of the phenomenon. The implications of fictional self-referentiality, the 'meanings' of metafiction, are disputed, so too are the delimitations of the genre. The very terms chosen to designate this type of fiction tend, as Robert Siegle (1986:2–4) points out, to reveal the critic's assumptions about the category. The 'self' in terms such as 'self-conscious' and 'self-reflexive' is frequently assimilated with a personal, human self, and 'introspective', 'introverted' and 'narcissistic' similarly create an anthropomorphic self for fiction. Not surprisingly, then, a number of critics have construed metafiction as a projection of the authorial self. 'Perhaps the great theme of the reflexive novel is provided by the question "Who is writing?"', writes Michael Boyd (1983:39). This seems unduly restrictive. The role of the author is indeed an important concern in many reflexive novels, but it is far from being the only one, and the 'self' metafiction examines is not a human, psychological entity but a number of linguistic and literary processes. It is also interesting to note that many of the terms chosen to designate reflexive fiction tend to carry negative connotations when used about human beings. Narcissism, introspection and even self-consciousness are frequently seen as disabling tendencies in a person, as an almost shameful preoccupation with self inhibiting active involvement with other people and with the world. As we have already seen, it is precisely this perception of self-involvement which has earned metafiction a bad name. The term 'antifiction' is problematic on another count; so, to some extent, is 'metafiction'. Both these labels suggest that the texts they refer to are *not* fiction but something else, in one case the very opposite of fiction, in the other a derivative, secondary kind of writing. As it is the aim of this book to argue that reflexivity is neither derivative, peripheral or disabling, but a central aspect of what constitutes fiction as fiction, I would perhaps be better advised to avoid all of these terms. It would appear, however, that 'metafiction' has established itself as the dominant designation for contemporary reflexive fiction, and so is the label most likely to be recognised. I have therefore decided to retain it, at least provisionally. Metafiction, the word and the genre, will be put 'under erasure' in this book, which means that they will be adopted for the purpose of scrutiny, but on the understanding that conditions may be revealed under which their existential basis must be put in doubt.

A glance at the definitions quoted at the beginning of this book reveals both continuities and differences in critical accounts of metafiction. Several of them refer to the relationship between fiction and reality. Metafiction 'flaunts its own condition of artifice' (Alter) and so breaks the mimetic illusion central to realist fiction. But what happens to fiction when it no longer pretends to reflect the real world? It examines the nature of the mimetic illusion itself, according to Robert Alter. It realises that the only reality for fiction is the reality of its own discourse, and so it transforms the process of writing into the subject of writing, argues Mas'ud Zavarzadeh. It refers to other fictions instead of to reality, writes Hans Skei. The 'self' of fiction, in Skei's formulation, is intertextual instead of mimetic. Michael Boyd reminds us of the close relationship between metafiction and literary theory and criticism. Metafiction presents a theory of fiction from within a fictional text and so blurs the distinction between primary and secondary writing, between fiction and writing about fiction. Hutcheon, McCaffery and Boyd stress metafiction's concern with language and story-telling processes. 'Reality', or 'the world', acquires a problematic status. If fiction can be the only reality for fiction, then any other reality would seem to be banished. Alter, Zavarzadeh and Skei represent the view that metafiction, in order to examine itself, must turn its back on everything that is external to it. But, as Waugh suggests, the fictionality of fiction may well have implications which go beyond the fictional universe. It is not only in novels that reality is 'transformed by and filtered through narrative assumptions and conventions' (McCaffery), but in a number of other discourses, many of which function to define (or construct) reality as we know it. 'Thus', writes the American novelist John Barth, 'Art is as natural an artifice as Nature; the truth of fiction is that Fact is fantasy; the made-up story is a model of the world' (1979:33). Or, as Linda Hutcheon once put it, 'Even nature . . . doesn't grow on trees' (1989:2). To many readers, and writers, such formulations, virtually conflating fiction and reality by completely ignoring the difference between the text and the world, are potentially misleading; it is essential, they claim, to retain some sense of what separates fact from fantasy, reality from fiction. The point nevertheless remains valid: metafiction serves as a reminder that everything in the human world is mediated through systems of representation. 'Reflexivity', writes Robert Siegle, 'is at the very least an essential means of keeping conventions marked as such' (1986:244).

The reflexive curve and the limits of metafiction

The word reflexivity, derived from the Latin *flectere*, to bend, signifies a bending back, or, among several other possibilities, a bending again. It is used in the language of grammar to indicate an identity between the subject and the object: a reflexive verb, a reflexive pronoun (see Ashmore, 1989:30–1). Michael Boyd illustrates the difference between 'ordinary' and reflexive denotation by means of two figures:

Figure 1   Figure 2

In denotation of the normal kind, the signifier 'tree' points outward, to its referent outside the signifying system. In the reflexive mode, the denotative arrow is arrested and turned back on the signifier: the 'subject' of the proposition is not the extratextual object but the signifying process itself (Boyd, 1983:38). Robert Siegle, on the other hand, proposes a model for the 'reflexive circuit' which, after turning around itself, continues on its way towards a signified outside of the text:

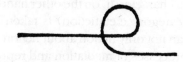

Figure 3

A rather ingenuous account of the etymology of the word 'reflex' (a double, not a single, turn), enables him to justify his view of fictional reflexivity as a mode of writing which turns on its own processes *in order to* signify something else (Siegle, 1986:2–3).

These etymological and graphical differences have important implications for our understanding of the phenomenon of reflexivity in fiction. Michael Boyd (1983:36) writes that in theory, all transitive verbs can become reflexive, but some actions seem necessarily reflexive—suicide and masturbation being cases in point. If we choose to take a restrictive view of fictional reflexivity and consider only actions, or texts, which seem 'naturally' or 'necessarily' reflexive, it is perhaps inevitable that the whole phenomenon becomes associated with acts of self-destruction or self-gratification. Not surprisingly, then, metafiction has frequently been associated with the 'death of the novel' which has been proclaimed with great regularity in the second half of the twentieth century. Whether masturbation was the direct cause of death is not always clear—what seems evident, however, is that this gloomy outlook is directly related to a narrow view of what the reflexive mode signifies for fiction. If we restrict the category 'reflexive fiction' to texts that are overt or explicit in their reflexive commentary, and the adjective 'reflexive' to statements about writing and art only, we impose serious limitations, not only on 'reflexivity' as such, but also on the fictional text's potential for meaning. It could mean arguing, for example, that John Fowles's narrator in *The French Lieutenant's Woman* ('I do not know. This story I am telling is all imagination. These characters I create never existed outside my own mind.' (Fowles, 1970:85)) would qualify as truly reflexive, whereas Peter Carey's in *Illywhacker* ('I am a terrible liar and I have always been a liar. I say that early to set things straight.' (Carey, 1986:11)) would not; *his* admission would be read as a statement about the narrator Herbert Badgery, not as a reference to the fictionality of *Illywhacker* itself and by implication to other tall tales about the Australian character. If, on the other hand, reflexivity (and by extension, the category metafiction) is taken to have a wider significance, to mean not only fiction about fiction but fiction about fictional systems, processes of mediation and representation in the text and elsewhere, the genre becomes a very large one indeed, hardly distinguishable, some might argue, from that of 'fiction' itself.

Writing about the sociology of scientific knowledge, Steve Woolgar (1988) defines reflexivity as the relationship between representation and represented object. Does the object constitute the representation or the other way around? he asks. A reflexive practice, in his formulation, is one which questions the 'ideology of representation' common to scientific discourse and realist fiction. One may wish to argue that the two disciplines, science and fiction, are too different for reflexivity to have the same implications for both. In scientific discourses, a rhetoric of realism (disregard for the signifying process) normally serves to enhance the truth-value (scientific status) of a statement; reflexivity, by suggesting that the scientific object may be constituted not independently of, but *through* the processes of representation, thus serves to qualify its truth-value, to make it culturally and discursively relative. In fiction, on the other hand, truth is always relative. By identifying itself as a fiction, a text is already, reflexively, setting itself apart from 'true' stories about the world. Overtly reflexive texts merely remind us of what we already know: it is the text that constitutes the 'world' of the fiction, not the other way around. But this difference is perhaps not as great as it seems. The fictionality of stories and characters does not mean that fictional representation functions in ways fundamentally different from representation in the real world. Language mediates our perception of both fiction and reality, so do a number of other codes and systems of representation. The reflexive mode in fiction, calling attention to these processes, serves to problematise the ways in which we gain access to knowledge of all kinds. Sociologists such as Steve Woolgar, Malcolm Ashmore and Michael Mulkay have introduced into scientific writing the reflexive modes which they call the 'new literary forms', arguing that true stories about the world, in order to be 'true', must be self-conscious, must acknowledge the story-telling process. The implication of their work, for fiction, is the same as that of Robert Siegle's reflexive circuit: reflexivity represents a mode of access, via fiction, to the world.

Three models for metafiction

In 'The Novelist at the Crossroads' David Lodge (1977:105) identifies four categories in contemporary fiction: the novel, the non-fiction novel, the fabulation and the problematic novel. 'Novel' here refers to the realist novel, and by 'problematic' he means reflexive.

Few critics would go so far as to situate metafiction *outside* the genre of the novel, but Lodge's classification is nevertheless characteristic of a dominant tendency in the theorising of fiction: the novel, it has been assumed, has a 'natural' affinity with the mode of realism, and all other modes (fantasy, metafiction, avant-garde) must be regarded as dissident sub-genres, situating themselves in opposition to the dominant mode of realism. In her excellent book *Fantasy and Mimesis* Kathryn Hume argues that this view has imposed serious restrictions on our understanding of literary texts: mimesis and fantasy, she claims, are complementary, not mutually exclusive impulses in fiction. The next chapter of this book will examine the relationship between mimesis and reflexivity in order to show that the perceived opposition between these two modes is equally illusory. In the present context the important point is that a great many accounts of metafiction have seen this category, or genre, as primarily a reaction against realist writing and a denial of the mimetic enterprise. Thus Robert Alter, in *Partial Magic*, writes a history of the novel based on the assumption that reflexivity is the dominant function whenever realism is at a low ebb, and vice versa. Reflexivity, he argues, was important to the novel in the early stages of its development (Cervantes, and particularly eighteenth-century writers such as Sterne, Fielding and Diderot), but was completely eclipsed as realism became the dominant mode in the nineteenth century. In the early parts of this century, modernist experimentation did *not*, according to Alter, fundamentally disturb the realist function; modernist fiction obeys the logic of psychological realism, not reflexivity. It was only later, with writers like Beckett, Nabokov and Borges, that fiction again turned resolutely towards the reflexive 'pole', and the postmodern period has, of course, been the high point for the reflexive novel, so high, in fact, that many critics now regard it as having reached a point of metafictional exhaustion.

Alter here exemplifies what I will call the first critical model for metafiction: metafiction-as-genre, or metafiction as anti-mimesis. Apart from the emphasis on metafiction's repudiation of realism, the model is most typically characterised by the various restrictions imposed on the genre of what Alter calls self-conscious fiction. Realist fiction is denied its self-conscious dimension: Alter discusses at length possible contenders from the nineteenth century (Melville,

Thackeray), only to dismiss them. Even more problematically, he excludes modernist writers such as Conrad and Woolf. In order for a text to be classified as a metafiction, he argues, reflexivity must be a dominant, not an intermittent tendency, and it must be clearly and overtly stated. Excluding anything but the most explicitly self-conscious fictions, Alter and critics who share his views make of metafiction a small and rather peripheral genre. Some would like to confine it to contemporary ('postmodern') fiction only; some would prefer to use the term exclusively to designate the group of American writers (Barth, Barthelme, Coover, Gass, etc.) for whom it was initially employed. Not all texts about writing and art are included: Michael Boyd (1983:31), for example, writes that the 'novel of the artist' need not be reflexive. Neither is all anti-realist fiction metafictional: extreme types of experimental writing tend to be excluded. Patricia Waugh (1984:12) argues that 'aleatory fiction' (texts which 'set out to resist the normal processes of reading, memory and understanding') go too far in their anti-mimetic enterprise: unlike metafiction, they do not subvert the conventions of realism, but simply ignore them. Common among many commentators is the view that contemporary metafiction is a short-term trend: it will soon have exhausted the possibilities of self-scrutiny and so must either die or mutate into new and more vigorous forms.

No wonder, perhaps, that it has been possible to say 'awful things' about metafiction. The problem, of course, with a restrictive, generic definition is that it has very little to say about the phenomenon of reflexivity itself and how it affects our reading of literary texts. Why should one want to dismiss intermittent and less overtly reflexive commentary, which, we must assume, is no less reflexive than the explicit varieties, and so has to be considered as meaningful when it occurs? Separating metafiction from 'mainstream' novelistic practice seems destined to impoverish both. Metafiction becomes a kind of aberration, intriguing and amusing, perhaps, but unimportant, and the mainstream novel is denied the important insights afforded by a reflexive enquiry: a scrutiny of its status as a linguistic and narrative artefact; an examination of how the 'real' is constructed, both in fiction and in the world; a recognition, finally, of the roles of representation and mediation in any object or text perceived as meaningful.

Speculating about the reasons for the critical marginalisation of reflexivity, the Norwegian critic Hans Skei writes:

> Can we then imagine that while the form of the novel continued to develop, the theories surrounding it solidified at a given point in time in the last century, and that that explains something of the hostility towards experimental or metafictional literature? New experimentation is by many judged in negative terms in relation to a narrow concept of realism. (Skei, 1987:15; translation mine)

The 'narrow concept of realism' which has haunted the theory of fiction stems from a belief that it is possible for art to simply 'mirror' or imitate the real. The realists, writes Alison Lee, 'appear to have wanted to create a formula for the literal transcription of reality into art' (1990:5). According to the views of the French naturalist movement, art should aspire to the status of a science, an objective instrument for examining society. One of the consequences of this theory of art was that the work of art had to become self-effacing: in order to prove the 'reality' of the represented world it became necessary to pretend that the medium (language, canvas, artistic conventions) did not exist. The metaphors employed by the theorists of realism describe the function of art in terms of transparency and neutral instrumentality: the novel is a 'slice of life', a 'window on the world', or, in Stendhal's famous formulation, 'a mirror journeying down the high road'.

Disregarding everything that makes the work of art distinctive, this rather naive theory of literary realism does not equip us very well to read any kind of fiction, not even that of the realist tradition. It certainly seems entirely inadequate for dealing with the explicitly anti-mimetic modes of twentieth-century literature. Its survival into the late twentieth century does not so much prove its validity as point to the historical circumstances surrounding the constitution of the novel as a genre: from being a relatively recent, minor and undertheorised genre, the novel in the nineteenth century developed into the dominant form of literary art. The 'triumph' of the novel is therefore linked to the prevailing mode of nineteenth-century fiction, realism. The history and theory of the novel in this respect contrasts with those of other literary forms, such as poetry or drama. These forms have a longer generic history; they are not regarded as products of realism. Not surprisingly, then, the reflexive dimension has been accommodated fairly easily into their generic make-up: critics have not to the same extent considered it necessary to create sub-genres (meta-poetry, meta-theatre) to account for, say, the poetry of Mallarmé and Stevens, or the drama of Pirandello and Beckett.

While the theory of fiction, especially in English and American criticism, remained essentially mimetic, elsewhere, other theoretical approaches were developed which would allow for radically different ways of reading literary texts. Ferdinand de Saussure, a Swiss linguist teaching at the University of Geneva in the early years of this century, divided the linguistic sign into *signifier* (its written or spoken form) and *signified* (concept represented by the signifier), insisting that the relationship between the two is a purely arbitrary, conventional one. Linguistic meaning, according to Saussure, comes about through a system of similarity and difference, not through a natural affinity between signifier and signified. In eastern Europe, another group of linguists came together in what is now called the formalist movement. One of their central arguments was that there are important differences between ordinary language, which is referential, and literary language, which does not refer to anything in the world outside the text.

Half a century after the publication of Saussure's theories (*Course in General Linguistics*, published posthumously in 1915), the French philosopher Jacques Derrida, building on, but going beyond Saussurian linguistics, insisted that western thinking from Plato to the present (and including Saussure) is grounded in a 'metaphysics of presence', a belief in the existence, outside language, of an absolute reality (an 'ultimate referent') serving to organise the linguistic system and to determine meaning. Derrida's famous axiom 'there is nothing outside the text' signals the end of metaphysics: to him, it is not possible to get beyond the linguistic system in which both signifiers and signifieds partake in an ungrounded play of meanings. Textual meaning, to Derrida, is infinitely plural and irreducible; it cannot be reduced to any single extra-textual referent.

Neither Saussure nor Derrida are primarily concerned with literary texts, but their thinking has had a major impact on literary criticism. Structuralist criticism, inspired by Saussurean linguistics and by the Russian formalists, turned its attention away from the represented universe in an effort to explore the role of the signifier in the literary experience. If literary meaning is the product of linguistic and literary systems, the task of the critic becomes that of examining these systems to discover how meaning is generated. 'Literature had long enough been regarded as a message without a code for it to become necessary to regard it for a time as a code without a message', writes Gérard Genette (1982:7). Deconstructionist criticism, which is based on Derrida's theorising, *does* concern itself with the nature of textual meaning, but meaning as plural and unstable, always escaping any attempt to pin it down or to locate a stable referent outside the text. Deconstructing the text generally means showing how the text deconstructs itself, how it undermines its own claims to coherence and intelligibility.

In the light of these theoretical approaches, a purely mimetic reading of fiction becomes an impossibility: the one thing a literary text *cannot* do is imitate or reflect the world through a mirror-like, self-effacing medium. The 'mirror' blurs, reference and meaning become indeterminate and the elaborate games of the signifying system become the focus of attention. To many formalists, structuralists and deconstructionists, the primary function of literature became *reflexive* rather than *reflective*. To the formalists, literary language is by its very nature self-referential: by setting itself apart from ordinary uses of language it draws attention to its own formal features and the relationships that are established between them. Literature, before it can be 'about' anything else, is primarily about itself. Viktor Shklovsky, one of the early members of the group, in his book *On the Theory of Prose* cites *Tristram Shandy*, perhaps the most overtly reflexive novel in the European tradition, as the archetype for *all* novels. His view, that literature is inevitably and essentially reflexive, has been echoed throughout twentieth-century literary theory, often by the most influential representatives of structuralist and post-structuralist (deconstructionist) criticism. Tzvetan Todorov, a structuralist, writes:

> Through its web of events, every work, every novel, tells the story of its own creation, its own story. Works like those of Laclos

or Proust merely make explicit a truth which underlies all literary creation. Thus appears the futility of searching for the final meaning of a novel, or a play; the meaning of a work consists in telling about itself, in speaking about its own existence. (Todorov, 1967:49; translation mine)

And Paul de Man, one of the main exponents of literary deconstruction:

> The self-reflecting mirror-effect by means of which a work of fiction asserts, by its very existence, its separation from empirical reality, its divergence, as a sign, from a meaning that depends for its existence on the constitutive activity of the sign, characterises the work of literature in its essence. (de Man, 1983:17)

To these critics, reflexivity is not an optional feature characterising a sub-genre of the novel; it is essential, the very element that distinguishes literature from ordinary uses of language. In their writing, another, and very different model for metafiction emerges: *all* fiction is metafiction, and the difference between *War and Peace* and *Tristram Shandy* is not one of *kind*, but merely of a lesser or greater explicitness in the metafictional awareness. Robert Siegle embraces such a model when he calls for an end to all restrictive and distorting definitions of fictional reflexivity:

> Giving up these misleading terms or definitions of reflexivity frees us to accept what we find when we carefully sift discussions of reflexivity and reflexive narratives themselves—that it is everywhere in narrative, in all periods and forms, sometimes explicit and sometimes implicit, always revealing the conceptual puddle over which fiction gallantly casts its narrative cloak so we can cross untroubled by the fluidity of our footing. (Siegle, 1986:4)

The advantage of this second model ('all fiction is metafiction') over the metafiction-as-genre model is that it allows for a comprehensive investigation of how reflexivity functions in all periods and all texts. Reflexivity, no longer marginalised or trivialised, becomes the key to the very nature of the literary artefact, and by extension, to the ways in which language and narrative structure human artefacts outside the literary text. But there are also potential disadvantages to an all-embracing model for metafiction. First, it may create problems for the literary historian: reflexivity can no longer be seen as a variable, prominent in certain periods and certain texts and absent in others. This could mean, for example, that the historian of French literature would be unable to make use of the the reflexive dimension to differentiate between Émile Zola and the *nouveau roman*, and the student of Australian literature could not make reflexivity a criterion for distinguishing Murray Bail from Henry Lawson. Another potential difficulty about affirming that all fiction is reflexive is that it can lead to a total dismissal of the mimetic function of literature. The criticism and theory inspired by structuralism and post-structuralism has frequently been accused of having no regard for mimesis or meaning; the literary text, in these readings, becomes pure form without content. Saussure's insistence on language as a self-contained system, formalism's distinction between literary and ordinary language and Derrida's 'there is nothing outside the text' could be taken to mean that no links can exist between literature and reality, or even that 'reality' as we know it does not exist. All of literature thus stands in danger of being regarded as irrelevant and disabling: the 'prisonhouse of language,' as Fredric Jameson terms it, preventing an active involvement with the world of political, psychological and social realities (see Jameson, 1972).

A departure from a naively mimetic view of the literary text does not, however, have to imply that the mimetic function is denied. And an interest in linguistic and narrative structures does not have to exclude other concerns—on the contrary. The 'danger' associated with the view that all fiction is reflexive is only there if reflexivity itself is taken in the narrow sense to mean nothing but literary introspection. It is preferable, therefore, to employ a more broadly relevant definition of the term, and to be aware that while the language of the literary text is different from ordinary language in many ways, there are other ways in which the two are remarkably similar. We do not altogether put aside our understanding of how words function in their everyday use when we come across them in a work of fiction, and so their 'ordinary' referential meaning is still operational, alongside our knowledge that the text is not referential in the normal sense. We do not really shut out the world when we read a literary text; the world enters through the back door, trapped by the very textuality through which literature seemingly excludes it out front.

The difficulty of deciding whether reflexivity is genre-specific or a quality essential to all literary language has made theorists cautious about specifying the extent of the reflexive enterprise. 'It may be the case', writes Michael Boyd, 'that all novels are at least partially reflexive' (1983:16), but he leaves this possibility largely unexplored, and concentrates on texts in which reflexivity is a dominant function. Patricia Waugh, while on the one hand adhering to a generic definition of metafiction, on the other insists that it is also 'a tendency or function inherent in *all* novels' (1984:5). In formulations such as these, reflexivity is represented as a latent dimension in fiction, always present, but not always making itself obvious. It may be 'the "original condition" of the novel as a genre' (Hutcheon, 1984:8) or 'that which gives the novel its identity' (Waugh, 1984:5) but it is often obscured by other functions and so not truly present to the reader.

If a text's latent reflexivity is to be activated, if a text is to be read as a metafiction, the onus, finally, is on the reader. Certain texts, such as John Fowles's *Mantissa*, are so explicit in their reflexive commentary that the reader would find it hard to ignore this dimension; others, however, are much less obviously metafictional, and so depend on a 'metafictional competence' in the reader to be realised as such. A metafictional competence consists, first of all, in an awareness that literary texts *may* refer to themselves as linguistic and narrative systems. One does not, of course, have to know about concepts such as 'reflexivity' and 'metafiction' in order to interpret a text reflexively, but the history of literary criticism does not throw up many examples of reflexive readings before the time when such terms, and the concepts they refer to, had become current. With the exception of the Russian formalists, few critics paid much attention to reflexivity in fiction until the second half of the twentieth century. It is hardly surprising, however, that the contemporary period has experienced an unprecedented interest in fictional reflexivity. The intellectual climate which produced structuralism and post-structuralism in literary criticism has also pro-duced an awareness of signifying systems in other disciplines, and the need to theorise one's practices has been felt throughout a wide range of disciplines. Reflexivity has become a central concept in the movement known as postmodernism—one of the few elements, in fact, most theories of postmodernism seem to agree on. In literary studies, the last twenty years or so have seen literary theory become an essential part of the literary experience; almost anybody who has studied literature in this period will have been in contact with some aspect of literary theory. The theoretically literate reader is the reader most likely to seek out moments when the literary text theorises itself, reflexive moments, when the difference between fiction and theory, between fiction and criticism, becomes blurred, and the text echoes the reader's own preoccupations. It is academic criticism which is most likely to produce reflexive readings; reviewers and critics writing for a 'general' rather than an academic audience are much less interested in interpreting novels as metafictions—in fact it is not uncommon for such critics to dismiss the whole reflexive dimension as theoretical hair-splitting, and to regard explicitly reflexive novels as poor fiction.

The favourite subject matter for reflexive criticism is the postmodern novel. This type of fiction can perhaps be seen to have a natural affinity with theoretically informed criticism: it is the product of the same moment in intellectual history, the same impulses and preoccupations. Indeed, it has often been noted that many writers of postmodern fiction (John Barth, Umberto Eco, Christine Brooke-Rose, for example) are themselves academics and literary theorists. But reflexive readers have also sought out the forerunners of postmodern fiction, and found them in Fielding, Sterne, Joyce, Proust and Woolf. Moreover, reflexive reading practices have been brought to bear on texts belonging to other traditions, even that of realist fiction: Roland Barthes and Ross Chambers have both reread Balzac's 'Sarrasine' reflexively, showing how through an embedded story-telling scene it thematises its own effect on the reader; Leo Bersani (among others) has read *Madame Bovary* as a critique of the very concept of literary realism. Michael Boyd comments:

> We should not miss the irony of the situation: The most famous creation of the father of realism turns out to be a parody of both the heroines of realistic novels and of the women who identify with such heroines. Flaubert, while working within the norms of

realism, has managed to subvert that realism by making it look at itself instead of at the world. (Boyd, 1983:35–6)

In this reflexive rereading of realist classics, a third model for metafiction emerges, an alternative to the generic as well as the all-embracing model: metafiction is the product of a certain practice of *reading*, a particular kind of attention brought to bear on the fictional text. All texts can be read as metafictions, but in order for this potential to be realised, the reader has to bring to the text a certain kind of interest, a set of expectations and a specific competence. The contemporary academic reader, reading the literary tradition from the perspective of literary theory and postmodern fiction, 'recreates' that tradition in reflexive robes, finds metafictions where previous readers found nothing but social realism, psychological realism, or fantasy. If read in accordance with reader-response theories such as those of Stanley Fish (1980), who insists that textual meaning is the product of the act of reading alone, not of the text, this model could be made to suggest that the reflexivity of a text is entirely dependent on the reader's input. The reflexive reading, then, would be produced independently of any textual feature guiding the reader in that direction. If on the other hand we wish to retain a sense of the text itself guiding our interpretative activities, the reader-oriented model for metafiction may still be of value. Adopted more cautiously, it explains how the context of reception will determine which textual features are privileged, which intertextual connections explored and which lines of interpretation followed.

Is it necessary, or even desirable, to make a choice between the three models for metafiction outlined here? On the one hand, my answer would be that it isn't: in order to explore the function of reflexivity in contemporary texts and contemporary critical debates one needs to be aware of the different ways the term and the concepts connected with it have circulated. On the other hand, it is impossible for any criticism, and certainly for this critic, to adopt a position of passive neutrality towards the object of one's research. If fiction, in its reflexive guise, is criticism, criticism cannot in its turn avoid the inward gaze: it must scrutinise its own brand of story-telling. The story *this* book is trying to tell is about metafiction—or so, at least, the title tells us (although the questionmark suggests a certain hesitancy). Knowing the important role of titles as framing devices, one will perhaps conclude that the book advertises itself as a *generic* study, concerned to describe a particular kind of contemporary text. And of course it *is* a generic study, but in the sense that the genre 'metafiction' and the history of its constitution form part of its subject matter. It will not, for reasons outlined above, adopt a narrow generic definition, nor will it accept the view of metafiction as a period concept, only applicable to late twentieth-century fiction. The two other models proposed here, the one all-embracing, the other reader-oriented, are both more compatible with my understanding of how reflexivity affects the literary experience, but they have drawbacks of their own, not least of which is the fact that my object of study seemingly dissolves under their scrutiny and ceases to be distinctive. The logical problem facing the critic who wishes to have her metafiction and deconstruct it too in many ways echoes that of the Cretan liar and is no more likely to find a satisfactory solution. Forced to examine, reflexively, our critical conscience and its various assumptions and paradoxes, we may have arrived at a theoretical impasse. It is also possible, however, that we have found a position from which the lies, ambiguities and insights of metafiction can be productively inter-preted and enjoyed.

Metamimesis

Words, images and things: Magritte and Robbe-Grillet

Figure 4

René Magritte's famous painting of a pipe carrying the inscription 'This is not a pipe' points to modes of representation in both language and the visual arts, reflexively highlighting conventional relationships between the two. First, the apparent contradiction between image and text calls attention to the obvious fact that the painting, however much it *resembles* a pipe, can never *be* a pipe: it belongs to the realm of pseudo-objects which, while striving to imitate the world of real things, are nevertheless confined to the secondary status of representations. Originally accompanied by the title 'The use of words', the painting moreover questions the correspondence between *words* and the things they supposedly designate. Not only is the short sentence itself not a pipe; it does not refer to a real pipe. But then, perhaps it should not be assumed that the inscription refers to the painted image at all: image and sentence exist independently of real referents; they also exist independently of each other. Michel Foucault, in his short monograph on Magritte also entitled *This Is Not a Pipe*, argues that this is a painting which instructs its viewers to reconsider the relationship between words, images and things, teaching them to see/read outside the conventions of visual and verbal representation:

> We do not see the teacher's pointer, but it rules throughout— precisely like his voice, in the act of articulating very clearly, 'This is a pipe.' From painting to image, from image to text, from text to voice, a sort of imaginary pointer indicates, shows, fixes, locates, imposes a system of references, tries to stabilize a unique space. But why have we introduced the teacher's voice? Because scarcely has he stated, 'This is a pipe,' before he must correct himself and stutter, 'This is not a pipe, but a drawing of a pipe,' 'This is not a pipe but a sentence saying that this is not a pipe,' 'The sentence "this is not a pipe" is not a pipe,' 'In the sentence "this is not a pipe," *this* is not a pipe: the painting, written sentence, drawing of a pipe—all this is not a pipe.' (Foucault, 1983:29–30)

The verb 'to represent' is generally understood to mean 'to stand for', in other words to symbolise something which is absent. But to represent also means to 'make present', to somehow restore the absent object to the mind and the senses. During the period of what Foucault in *The Order of Things* (1970) refers to as the 'classical episteme' (the seventeenth and eighteenth centuries) representation was conceived as offering direct access to objects outside the representing system. The medium of representation (the signifier) was regarded as transparent, and, as such, subordinate to the signified entity whose existence it merely served to confirm. 'The model for this idea of representation', writes Paul de Man, 'is the painted image, restoring the object to view as if it were present and thus assuring the continuation of its presence' (1983:123). The 'age of representation,' according to Foucault, gave way in the nineteenth century to the modern episteme ('episteme' is his name for the fundamental cultural code underlying social and artistic practices), which blurs the perfect transparency of the signifier and makes of the medium an object of study in its own right: 'The threshold between Classicism and modernity . . . had been definitively crossed when words ceased to intersect with representations and to provide a spontaneous grid for the knowledge of things' (Foucault, 1970:304). In twentieth-century visual art, painters like Klee and Kandinsky marked their departure from the representational realism of classical art by declaring the independence of the work of art: their work is autonomous, and so does not seek to represent or imitate anything in the outside world. The position of Magritte in this context is ambiguous. On the surface, it would seem that he adheres to the classical tradition of faithful, literal transcription: his paintings reproduce the real with an almost photographic accuracy. But paintings like 'This is not a pipe' undermine representation from within, cite conventions of representation only to reverse their logic. The effect, finally, complements that of modernist abstraction: 'In order to deploy his plastic signs, Klee wove a new space. Magritte allows the old space of representation to rule, but only at the surface, no more than a polished stone, bearing words and shapes: beneath, nothing' (Foucault, 1983:41). In another painting, 'La lunette d'approche' (1963), Magritte directly addresses the view of art as a transparent 'window on the world': a window frames the view of a clouded skyscape, but part of the window opens to reveals a black void beyond. The represented 'world' does not exist except as a function of the window; it comes into being through the act of representation.

The relationship between words and things and the various rules governing the representational game have captured the imagination of writers from classical Greece to the postmodernist era. Like Magritte, many of them examine the notion of representation from within the very conventions they challenge and so end up making a statement not about a reality external to the work of art but about the work of art itself and its pseudo-representational status. Visual representation has become a frequent motif for this type of metafiction. Like language governed by conventions, but unlike language in that it is based on a relationship of resemblance with the represented object, the visual image is generally regarded as offering more immediate access to real things. By representing, in language, the act of 'reading' an image which in its turn represents something else, reflexive texts open the door to a great range of speculations on the nature of representation, its possibilities, its assumptions, its paradoxes.

Alain Robbe-Grillet's writing is frequently described as 'a painting in motion'. His texts juxtapose elements of visual and verbal representation: pictorial 'stills' and narrative movement are combined, or, rather, played against each other in a manner which unsettles the representative process, blurring the distinction between representation and illusion. The short story 'The Secret Room', first published in 1962, exemplifies such a procedure.

The very last word of 'The Secret Room', 'canvas', confirms what the reader has suspected throughout: the sacrificial murder described in the story is not 'real'; it 'takes place' in a painting. References to pictorial representation abound: the story is dedicated to Gustave Moreau, a surrealist painter; it is part of a collection entitled *Snapshots* (*Instantanés* in the original French). The story opens on the words 'The first thing to be seen' and what can 'be seen' on the canvas is all it tells us. The scene is described in minute detail, often in the vocabulary of the visual arts: geometric shapes, formal arrangement, distribution of colour. We become aware of someone in the act of viewing, a human source for the story's perspective. The narrator's eyes move around the canvas, focusing on detail or 'standing back' to take in the full scene. When the visual surface is ambiguous he has to make conjectures : the cloth under the victim's head is 'perhaps' velvet, certain colours 'seem' to dominate. Teasingly, the story evokes conventions of visual representation: seemingly unaware of the laws of perspective the narrator describes the steps of the staircase as 'wide and deep' at the bottom but at the top reduced to 'a steep, narrow flight of steps' (Robbe-Grillet, 1968:67–8). The scene is seemingly static, immobile, depicted in the present tense. When movement *does* occur, our expectations are jolted. The chronology, however, is far from 'natural': the story is composed of a series of 'stills' (snapshots or *instantanés*) taking us backwards in time. We first see the murderer near the top of the stairway, then on the first step, then close to the body immediately after the act, and finally the murder itself is depicted. The concluding scene reverts to a 'normal' chronology: the man is once again at the top of the stairs, then he is gone. Hesitating between pictorial and narrative representation, the story alerts the reader to connections between the two. Pictures tell 'stories' in spite of their immobility, and narratives contain descriptive scenes where time apparently stands still. The 'reader' of a painting such as the one described supplies the narrative element, imagines the scene of the murder from the clues present in the picture. The reader of a literary narrative, on the other hand, is not unaccustomed to distorted chronologies: flashbacks to 'past' events followed by a narrative progression which eventually brings us back to the initial point in time belong to standard story-telling practices, and would normally not be received as 'unnatural' at all. At once familiar and unfamiliar, conventional and distorted, the techniques of 'The Secret Room' have the effect of denaturalising and thus drawing our attention to conventions which otherwise go unnoticed, seemingly giving access to an imagined 'real' beyond the representational game.

It is, of course, not only in terms of the purely technical aspects of depiction and narration that Robbe-Grillet in this story draws on conventional modes of representation. The melodramatic scene is composed entirely of stock elements in gothic horror: the elegant and mysterious murderer and his beautiful young victim, the exotic setting of vaulted archways, rich fabrics, chains and incense. The reader/viewer is on familiar territory: this is a story of mystery, horror, passion, violence, and above all, sex. The 'reality' of the scene is entirely intertextual, shaped by other fictions, other images and certain conventional modes of seeing and reading. It is *so* conventional that it flaunts its cliché-ridden surface, forcing the reader to acknowledge a certain complicity in its construction. The barely disguised presence of the viewer/narrator in the story alerts us to the fact that representation comes about through the interaction between textual conventions and conventions of reception. What is the role of the viewer in 'The Secret Room', we may wonder. Is he a passive recorder or does he construct/fantasise the elements in the painting/story? Why, *my* reader may ask, do I persist in referring to the anonymous viewer as 'he'? The manner in which the characters are described leaves little doubt. The dead woman is described as 'a white body whose full, supple flesh can be sensed, fragile, no doubt, and vulnerable' (Robbe-Grillet, 1968:66). Her exposed sex is 'provocative, proffered, useless now' (ibid.:67). The narrator identifies with the murderer to the point of projecting his emotions on to him: 'The man's posture allows his face to be seen only in a vague profile, but one senses in it a violent exultation, despite the rigid attitude, the silence, the immobility' (ibid.:70). The passive, seemingly objective narrative voice disguises an intense emotional involvement in the scene which clearly identifies it, and the tradition it belongs to, as male sexual fantasy. It does not matter whether there is one painting or several, or whether the painting is there in the first place. What matters is that 'The Secret Room' enacts and exposes a mode of representation which is both conventional and ideologically constructed. In *Ways of Seeing* John Berger argues that depictions of female nudes always imply a male viewer:

> In the average European oil painting of the nude the principal protagonist is never painted. He is the spectator in front of the picture and he is presumed to be a man. Everything is addressed to him. Everything must appear to be the result of his being there. It is for him that the figures have assumed their nudity. But he, by definition, is a stranger—with his clothes still on. (Berger, 1972:54)

Reflexivity in 'The Secret Room' functions to lay bare the conventions of representation in a number of ways. Like Magritte's pipe it works to denaturalise techniques of representation, forcing the reader to concentrate on the representational surface instead of passing 'through' it to the represented. But the represented in turn calls attention to itself as a construct, inviting an investigation into the conventions, artistic as well as cultural, which contribute to its making. Ironically, it is the very artificiality of the story-telling which prevents us from simply dismissing the whole scene as melodramatic and thus 'unrealistic': the impassive voice and the backward narrative momentum have the effect of enhancing rather than trivialising the climax (narrative *and* sexual) and its gruesome reality of rape and murder.

Literature and truth: ideologies of representation

'Is not the most naïve form of representation *mimesis*?' asks Jacques Derrida (1978:234). The concept of art as mimesis, or imitation, has been a constant in western civilisation since Plato, and, according to Derrida, its assumptions have governed critical theory to the present: 'the whole history of the interpretation of the arts of letters has moved and been transformed within the diverse logical possibilities opened up by the concept of *mimesis*' (Derrida 1981a:187). Mimesis inevitably involves art in a process of *truth*: by duplicating, copying a reality which precedes it, literature works in the service of truth, but truth cannot reside in the work of art itself, which merely borrows its truth-value from the entity it imitates to the extent that it is a faithful reproduction. In the Platonic system, and the Aristotelian aesthetic theory which derives from it, the origin of the written word is always to be found elsewhere, in a reality or truth which exists beyond representation as pure self-presence. According to such an ideology of representation (Derrida's 'metaphysics of presence'), the written word is in fact devalued. It is regarded as doubly derivative: writing imitates speech which in its turn symbolises what is real and true (mental activity, objects). Speech (*logos*), unlike writing, enjoys a privileged relationship with the real: the immediacy of the voice lends it an authenticity which the written symbol can never achieve. Within this system of logocentrism, where writing is conceived as debased speech, literary mimesis is frequently regarded with mistrust, its double remove from reality implying a greater potential for falsification. Plato thus banned poets, writers of 'falsehood', from his ideal republic, a gesture which is repeated whenever literature is condemned because it is insufficiently true to a reality which supposedly precedes it.

'It is an astonishing tribute to the eloquence and rigor of Plato and Aristotle as originators of western critical theory', writes Kathryn Hume, 'that most subsequent critics have assumed mimetic representation to be the essential relationship between text and the real world' (1984:5). The idea of mimetic representation has not, as Foucault demonstrates, remained static (or unquestioned) from its inception to our time, but the writing and critical theory of the twentieth century has questioned its foundations systematically, mounting a radical challenge to its basic assumption of literature as imitation. Re-examining the Platonic inheritance in an effort to uncover the presuppositions governing literary practices in western cultures, contemporary writers consider the possibility of going beyond mimesis to different modes of reading and writing.

In his article 'Frontiers of Narrative', first published in 1966, the French critic Gérard Genette compares Plato's account of literary modes and mimesis with that of Aristotle. Both, he argues, make the distinction between narrative and dramatic modes, and both value the dramatic mode (tragedy) over narrative because of its greater powers of imitation. The difference between the two is that Plato denies the quality of imitation, and so the label mimesis, to narrative, whereas Aristotle makes narrative (diegesis) a sub-category of mimesis. This difference, Genette argues, is superficial: both view narrative as an attenuated, weakened form of literary representation, inferior to a direct, dramatic presentation of words and action. But, as Genette shows, there are several problems with this way of thinking. Direct imitation of discourse is not so much imitation as tautology: 'the only thing that language can imitate perfectly is language, or, to be more precise, a discourse can imitate perfectly only a perfectly identical discourse; in short, a discourse can imitate only itself' (Genette, 1982:132). To reproduce discourse perfectly is not to imitate but to repeat, and in the case of a literary text, where what is represented is merely a simulated reality, the discourse is not repeated or imitated so much as constituted. If literary imitation on the other hand is understood as 'the fact of representing by verbal means a non-verbal reality' (ibid.:131), only imperfect imitation, or narrative, qualifies as mimetic discourse. The Platonic and Aristotelian conception of mimesis, and its attendant marginalisation of diegesis, evaporate: '*Mimesis* is *diegesis*' (ibid.:133).

Genette is well aware that to challenge the assumptions under-lying the most naive idea of literary representation may entail a wholesale rejection of the theory of mimesis, according to which the text functions as a simulacrum of reality. At the end of his article he examines contemporary French fiction and speculates on the possibility that it spells the death of the mimetic mode: 'It is as if literature had exhausted or overflowed the resources of its repre-sentative mode, and wanted to fold back into the indefinite murmur of its own discourse. Perhaps the novel, after poetry, is about to emerge definitively from the age of representation' (ibid.:143).

The end to any residual notion of mimesis and the rebirth of literature as textual (and intertextual) play outside the jurisdiction of representation has become the utopian dream of much postmodern writing and post-structuralist criticism. The most prominent advocate of a textuality free from the 'burden' of representation is undoubtedly Roland Barthes, who brushes aside mimesis to celebrate textual spectacle and pure linguistic play:

> The function of narrative is not to 'represent', it is to constitute a spectacle still very enigmatic for us but in any case not of a mimetic order . . . Narrative does not show, does not imitate; the passion which may excite us in reading a novel is not that of a 'vision' (in actual fact, we do not 'see' anything). Rather it is that of meaning, that of a higher order of relation which also has its emotions, its hopes, its dangers, its triumphs. 'What takes place' in a narrative is from the referential (reality) point of view literally *nothing*; 'what happens' is language alone, the adventure of language, the unceasing celebration of its coming. (Barthes, 1977:123–4)

To Barthes, the transition from mimesis to what he calls the 'writerly' text is not simply a question of aesthetic preference; the choice is ultimately ideological. He aligns mimesis with bourgeois society, whose characteristic it is to conceal the codes of its artefacts, presenting as natural what is culturally constructed. The mimetic text, especially that of the nineteenth-century realist tradition, centrally concerned to present its constructed illusion of reality as an unmediated 'slice of life' or 'window on the world', thus reinforces a system of control which works by hiding its agents. The writerly text, on the other hand, is presented as liberating because the reader is set free to take control of its destiny, and by implication, of her/his own. Barthes here joins Derrida and a number of theorists of metafiction in arguing that a critique of conventional modes of representation must imply a questioning of ideological assumptions inherent to them.

Like Barthes, Derrida celebrates the type of literary text (one might call it metafiction, although Derrida doesn't) which marks a departure from conventional modes of representation and holds up for scrutiny the categories 'truth' and 'literature' as constructed by the metaphysical tradition he associates with mimesis. But Derrida's idea of mimesis is far more complex, and he would never suggest that simply swapping realist for reflexive fiction would constitute a rupture with the logocentric ideology of representation. In fact, Derrida is at pains to refute the claims often made about deconstruction that it seeks to abolish reference, to demonstrate that there can be no such thing as an extra-textual reality and that the whole idea of representation in language should be abandoned:

> To distance oneself . . . from the habitual structure of reference, to challenge or complicate our common assumptions about it, does not amount to saying that there is *nothing* beyond language. (Quoted in Kearney, 1984:124)

> We must avoid having the indispensable critique of a certain naive relationship to the signified or the referent, to sense or meaning, remain fixed in a suspension, that is a pure and simple supression, of meaning or reference. (Derrida, 1981b:66)

The Platonic notion of mimesis, Derrida writes in *Dissemination*, is already a complex one. Before it can mean imitation, mimesis stands for the presentation of the thing itself. In this sense, mimesis is described as a 'writing on the soul', an inward revelation of truth as self-presence. As Christopher Norris points out, it is this second notion of mimesis which primarily concerns Derrida; it is here that he locates the metaphysics of presence which informs the Platonic system of representation (see Norris, 1987:55). By dismissing mimesis in the sense of imitation as *bad*, false mimesis, Plato institutes truth as revelation, presence, *logos*.

Juxtaposing Mallarmé's *Mimique* to Plato's *Philebus*, Derrida shows a text which seemingly functions outside the regime of mimesis: 'There is no imitation. The Mime imitates nothing. And to begin with, he doesn't imitate. There is nothing prior to the writing of his gestures' (Derrida, 1981a:194). By miming reference, imitating imitation, Mallarmé's text places itself outside the system of truth as reference to a lost origin. But it simultaneously works against the notion of truth as revelation: its resistance to any notion of thematic unity or overall meaning counteracts the kind of literary criticism which wants to recuperate it for Plato's other sense of mimesis as self-presence. In *Mimique* mimesis is not so much suspended as it is infinitely problematised, but it is precisely because the text cannot completely break with the representational assumptions of language that it works against a reification of the text itself as unique origin of meaning. By questioning the ideology of the mimetic enterprise Derrida in fact discovers a multiplication of mimetic traces:

> Perhaps, then, there is always more than one kind of *mimesis*; and perhaps it is in the strange mirror that reflects but also displaces and distorts one *mimesis* into the other, as though it were itself destined to mime or mask *itself*, that history—the history of literature—is lodged, along with the whole of its interpretation. (ibid.:191)

What sort of relevance can this Derridean critique have for our understanding of reflexivity and our reading of reflexive texts? What relationship, if any, can exist between the reflexive and the mimetic dimension of the text? According to a certain strain in post-structuralist criticism, reflexivity has simply replaced representation as the primary function of literature: with the suspension of reference, literature has become inward-looking. Instead of imitating the world, it imitates itself, in a kind of infinite circularity. 'The truth of our literature', writes Roland Barthes, 'is not in the practical order, but already it is no longer in the natural order: it is a mask which points to itself' (1972:98). The problem with such a view, however, is that it seems to endorse the reification of the text as self-presence, as revealed truth. A text which is *only* self-referential is a closed text, closed in the sense that it resists the pressure of external forces, closed also in that its potential for meaning is limited. This conception of the text is not one Barthes would have agreed with, but in his insistence on the unique reflexive 'truth' of literature and in numerous readings of texts as pure self-reflection lurks the shadow of the metaphysical heritage Derrida associates with Plato. Derrida's notion of a textual practice where mimesis remains operational, though reduced to a function which *mimes* rather than imitates an extra-textual reality, and where representation is multiplied and problematised, seems to account more aptly for the metamimetic critique at work in the reflexive text. No longer window on the world but circus or travelling fair, the text mimics life while marking its distance, its unrooted existence outside the laws of nature. At the same time, 'life' and 'nature' lose their metaphysical status and are seen to partake in the play of ungrounded textuality. Clowns, mimes and puppets perform feats of language and action, but although they are themselves insubstantial, their acts are haunted by reference, echoes of the various mimetic and ideological assumptions which inform the reality of readers and writers.

Realism and faith: phases of the reflexive image

'Representation', writes Jean Baudrillard, 'starts from the principle that the sign and the real are equivalent'. Simulation, on the other hand, 'starts from the Utopia of this principle of equivalence, *from the radical negation of the sign as value*, from the sign as reversion and death sentence of every reference' (Baudrillard, 1988:170). In the transition of the image from representation to simulation he distinguishes four phases:

1   It is the reflection of a basic reality.
2   It masks and perverts a basic reality.
3   It masks the *absence* of a basic reality.
4   It bears no relation to any reality whatever: it is its own pure simulacrum. (ibid.:170)

Phase 1, it would seem, characterises the mode of representation at work in non-fictional discourse and in realist fiction. There is an important difference, however: in fiction, the referent is not so much a 'basic reality' as itself a simulacrum. In order for fiction to function in accordance with Baudrillard's first phase, the 'suspension of disbelief' must operate in such a way as to blur the distinction between fiction and factual discourses. Phase 2 contains the development of literary criticism from Plato to our day: literature is a lie, a mask, a perversion. Whether its inability to match up to the real is deplored or celebrated, its *basis* is not questioned: literature is a function of reality, the real is the measure of its success or failure. In phase 3 the image is no longer ruled by reference: it still dissimulates, but what it masks is not so much reality as the absence of reality. Literature in a sense assumes the function of reality; it wills into existence a basis, an origin, which is not to be found elsewhere.

It is this generation of a real without origin that Baudrillard refers to as the 'hyperreal'. Phase 4, then, is perhaps merely hyperreality without the nostalgia for origins or truths, a celebration of intertextuality, self-reference and mimicry which has lost even the desire to ground the textual play in a hypothetical real.

Peter Carey's short story 'American Dreams' (in Carey, 1981:151–62) traces the transition from representation to hyperreality. To start with, there is a real town, and Mr Gleason secretly builds its miniature replica behind high walls on Bald Hill. After Mr Gleason's death, the walls are pulled down and the model town revealed, to the initial delight, but subsequent horror, of the townspeople. The image is *so* true to its origin that it even reveals what they do not want to know about themselves. As time passes, and the model town becomes a tourist attraction, the relationship between reality and replica is reversed. Tourists come down the hill to seek out people and places, taking photographs of the townspeople in poses exactly like those depicted by Gleason. When things start to change, and the townspeople no longer *look like* their images, they find that they have themselves *become* images: the simulacrum on the hill has become the 'reality' the town must model itself on. The next phase in the transformation of the image can only be conjectured: either the resemblance between real and copy will be abandoned and the image will have lost its representational function (become 'its own pure simulacrum'), or a nostalgic 'real' will be fabricated, modelled on the model, to mask the absence of a basic reality.

The leap from image to reality is, ultimately, a leap of faith, and the idea that images conceal nothing at all may lead to metaphysical despair. David Lodge's novel *How Far Can You Go?* follows Baudrillard's trajectory in its account of the Catholic faith, which it explicitly relates to faith in the mimetic illusion. When we first meet the novel's characters as young Catholic university students in the early 1950s, the narratives of the Bible are received by them as factual: the virgin birth and the resurrection are historical events, the basic reality upon which their faith is founded. Over the next thirty years they witness the gradual deconstruction of their metaphysical text. Historical accuracy is first questioned, then abandoned, and the Bible emerges in the domain of pure myth, symbolising Christian faith rather than representing reality. The question is, however, whether faith can survive the end of representation. With the suspicion that the imagery of their religion masks the absence of a metaphysical reality, the Catholics react in various ways. Some abandon their religion, some seek refuge in fundamentalist and mystical practices, others revert to earlier versions of their faith. Even outside the sphere of religion metaphysical anxiety affects belief in the representative power of narrative:

> So they stood upon the shores of Faith and felt the old dogmas and certainties ebbing away rapidly under their feet and between their toes, sapping the foundations upon which they stood, a sensation both agreeably stimulating and slightly unnerving. For we all like to believe, do we not, if only in stories? People who find religious belief absurd are often upset if a novelist breaks the illusion of reality he has created. (Lodge, 1980:142–3)

A world, and a literature, in which faith is redundant are presented as seductive but ultimately intolerable. The *alternative* to metaphysical despair or mindless religiosity seems in the end to be a kind of enlightened realism, affirmation of belief in reality (and God), but acknowledgement of the problematic status of the processes of representation. *How Far Can You Go?* functions according to the conventions of realist fiction in spite of its numerous reminders that it is 'just a fiction': *its* leap of faith consists in convincing the reader that its characters, however fictional, *stand for* real people to whom similar things happen. The text–world connection is affirmed, reality surviving its clash with hyperreality.

Angela Carter's *Nights at the Circus* stages another confrontation between real and hyperreal, but unlike *How Far Can You Go?* it does so from within the logic of simulation, not representation. In contrast to Lodge's retreat from the irrationality of the hyperreal, Carter presents a character who lives through the dementia of simulation in order to find a new reality, and a new self, on the far side. Mimetic faith here is not of the religious order; it is a confidence trick, and the laughter which rings through Siberia in the last pages of the novel expresses delight at having carried it off. 'To think I really fooled you!' (Carter, 1984:295) marvels Fevvers, winged freak and trickster, to her realist lover, perhaps also to the sceptical reader. Ironically, the deception turns out to be of very minor importance. Like Fevvers's virginity, the fictional illusion may not be intact, but love, knowledge and human 'truth', the things that really count, survive the demise of realist faith.

To Jack Walser, journalist and sceptic, Fevvers is initially one of the 'Great Humbugs of the World', a humbug he intends to expose. Unable to crack the hoax of the bird-woman and her witch-like protectress, he is eventually forced at least to consider the possibility that she is authentic. 'In a secular age', he ponders, 'an authentic miracle must purport to be a hoax, in order to gain credit in the world' (ibid.:17). Intrigued by Fevvers and her paradoxical status, he joins the circus as a clown, ostensibly to report on its fabricated magic, but also to explore the relationship between illusion and reality which, by now, he realises is more complex than he initially suspected. Donning the mask of the clown, he experiences a new freedom, 'the freedom to juggle with being' (ibid.:103), to play at appearances which resist the stubborn reality of the self. Clowns exist in the realm of hyperreality. They teach the truth about the world, but are themselves insubstantial, simulacra masking nothing: 'And what am I without my Buffo's face? Why, nobody at all. Take away my make-up and underneath is merely not-Buffo. An absence. A vacancy' (ibid.:122).

After the destruction of the circus in a train crash, Fevvers and Walser are separated, and their roles somehow reversed. Her wing broken, her magic lost, Fevvers faces the existential despair of her indeterminate status. Her desire for reality merges with her desire for Walser, but she wonders whether it is he who will 'turn out to be the beautiful illusion' (ibid.:245). Walser, deprived of his memory and his wits, eventually finds himself apprenticed to a crazed Shaman in an isolated community which does not recognise any difference between reality and illusion. To the villagers, Walser is himself a hallucination, a shared dream which nevertheless fits into their concept of the real. As he regains his reason, Walser realises that all notions of reality, including his own, depend on a certain relationship between knowledge and belief. Reunited, Fevvers and Walser share the experience of illusion and reality; they are now both part of the confidence trick and can laugh and despair at their place in the great cosmic joke.

Through a realism which bares its artifice (Lodge) or the mode of 'magic realism' (Carter), these two novels explore the nature of the mimetic illusion, and however different their outcome, both incorporate all the phases of Baudrillard's model, though not necessarily in his order. If, to Baudrillard, these phases have a certain fixed linearity, logical or chronological, in reflexive fiction reality and representation exist on a constantly changing ground. The text plays with, and is haunted by, conflicting mimetic modes, representing, miming or simulating a reality equally tainted by an unstable ontology.

Describing the reader's interaction with fictional representation, critics generally resort to well-rehearsed but undertheorised phrases such as 'willing suspension of disbelief', 'mimetic illusion' or 'mimetic faith'. These expressions are not quite synonymous: surely, to suspend disbelief is not exactly the same as to have faith, and the word illusion implies that someone (in most cases the reader him/herself) *knows* that it is an illusion. Although one does hear about spectators rushing on to the stage to rescue the heroine or readers contacting the author to find out what happened to a character after the end of the novel, one must assume that most readers, even back in the bad old mimetic days, were sufficiently sophisticated to know that fictions did not operate at a level of reality identical to their own. To assume that realist fiction functions according to the mode of representation at work in non-fictional discourse is to disregard the fact that the referent for fiction is *always* an illusion (and the reader knows it is) and is thus always already caught up in the logic of simulation. Exposing the illusion for what it is, in the manner of reflexive fiction, should therefore not be regarded as a destruction of essential faith; mimetic 'faith' always implies the knowledge of its own provisionality. On the other hand, to disregard the power of the mimetic illusion is also to misjudge the nature of the fictional experience. Its compelling, almost magical attraction has a way of surviving our knowledge that the magic is of the circus rather than the supernatural variety. 'When reading a novel', writes David Lodge, 'or writing one for that matter, we maintain a double consciousness of the characters as both, as it were, real and fictitious' (1980:240). This 'double consciousness' is not without conflicts. 'Illusion', writes Ernest Gombrich, 'is hard to describe or analyse, for though we may be intellectually aware of the fact that any given experience *must* be an illusion, we cannot, strictly speaking, watch ourselves having an illusion' (1972:5). The intellectual thrill afforded by metafiction is perhaps due precisely to the fact that it requires us, paradoxically, to watch ourselves having an illusion, to know that we are the subject of a confidence trick and nevertheless to continue to be taken in.

In the light of this close interaction between mimetic and reflexive impulses, it becomes difficult to sustain the common argument, referred to in the previous chapter, that realism and metafiction are mutually exclusive modes of writing. One could with equal justice maintain that the two are mutually dependent, for reflexivity is never more tied to the tradition of representation than when it most emphatically opposes it, and even the most conventional of realist fiction depends for its effect on the reader's awareness that its 'reality' is a fabricated one. In *Narcissistic Narrative* Linda Hutcheon, one of the most perceptive theorists of metafiction, distinguishes between, in the case of realism, a 'mimesis of product', and, in the case of metafiction, a 'mimesis of process'. But although her distinction avoids the fallacy of characterising metafiction as an anti-mimetic mode, it merely displaces the problem. The concept 'mimesis' cannot have the same meaning in each case, for the reflexive text does not so much *imitate* its own processes as examine them, holding up for scrutiny precisely the conventions and mechanisms that enable us to receive the text as mimesis. A more theoretically useful account of the interaction between mimesis and reflexivity in metafiction is offered by Brian McHale, who in *Postmodern Fiction* describes the struggle between conflicting modes of reception in terms of an 'ontological flicker'. The two modes are both available in the text, but cannot be apprehended at the same time. In order to switch from one to the other the reader adopts a different 'way of looking', a mental operation similar to that required by ambiguous visual images, such a Jastrow's duck/rabbit head or Escher's graphics of birds and fish. The reader *knows* that two levels of 'reality', illusion and non-illusion, are there in the text, but can only truly apprehend one at a time. It is this kind of complex reading practice which metafiction teaches, and once we are familiar with it, it becomes applicable also to texts that are not overtly reflexive. Reading backwards from contemporary texts, we are better able to appreciate the paradox of literary representation in the fiction of less problematic mimetic traditions.

The mode of realism does not imitate reality any more or less than other fictional modes; all fiction employs linguistic and literary conventions in order to produce particular effects and illusions, whether of a mimetic nature or not. The 'effect of reality' obtained in certain types of fiction depends on a number of factors, not least of which is the assumption of a shared mode of perception. This 'consensus reality' is a culturally relative concept, and it is therefore not infrequent to see one realism disputed in the name of another. When Virginia Woolf criticised the British realist writers Wells, Bennett and Goldsworthy she did so in the name of a kind of writing which in her view would be more true to life than theirs (see Woolf, 1966, 1975). Similarly, when Alain Robbe-Grillet in the 1950s attacked the psychological realism of modernist writers such as Woolf, he advocated another, ostensibly more objective way of representing the world (see Robbe-Grillet, 1965).

If most readers today do not associate either Woolf or Robbe-Grillet with realism, it is not because their writing fails to match a certain reality, it is because the word 'realism' is increasingly used as a period concept, referring to a particular tradition in fiction which became prominent in the nineteenth century and which still dominates most of what is being written, and read, today. The conventions of realism have not remained static, but as a number of them (such as the tendency to conceal fictionality) have become entrenched, they have become naturalised to the point where they are not perceived as conventions at all. What Michael Boyd calls the 'epistemological complacency' of realism stems from a tendency, within both texts and readers, to assimilate a particular tradition, to pass over its conventions as if they didn't exist and to believe that it offers access to an unmediated real. To Boyd (1983:18), as to a great many other critics and writers, mimetic faith in the realist text has become *bad* faith, a kind of conspiracy where the text pretends to be what it is not and the reader is all too willing to go along with the deceit. The danger with this kind of complacency is not just that we become bad, deluded readers, but that we might read the world itself as if it were a realist fiction. 'The motive for mimesis', writes Boyd, 'is to conceal from us the mediated, secondhand quality of our experience and to provide us with the easiest means of reassuring ourselves that we know the world' (ibid.:169).

By complicating the relationship between the concepts of fiction and reality, by violating the rules of mimetic representation, metafiction is not merely concerned to give us a lesson in literary theory. If the 'reality' we encounter in fiction is revealed to be an illusion, then its perceived resemblance to the world as we know it is still more disturbing. At some point we must begin to wonder whether the world itself could be tainted with the fictionality of fiction. Could *real* reality also be caught up in the logic of simulation?

Metahistories

The distinction between history and fiction seems clear enough: history is the story of *true* events, what actually happened, whereas fiction tells stories of a simulated reality. Whatever the validity of its simulated world, fiction, in terms of the real world, is a lie. The problem with this distinction is that it tends to fall apart when stories, and histories, are actually told. The history of the world, as we know it, is infused with fiction. Homeric and biblical narratives do not distinguish fact from myth, nor do they consider such a distinction valid, and the same can be said for most accounts of the past, both in western civilisation and in other cultural traditions. Shakespeare based his 'histories' on real events, but fictionalised them, and early novelists tended to disguise their fictions as 'histories'. The very word 'history' in English contains within it its fictional counterpart 'story', and many languages do not mark the difference between the two. Although the distinction between history and literature has been increasingly articulated in the western world since the Renaissance, it was with the development of history as a *science* in the nineteenth century that it became imperative: objective, verifiable accounts of the past could hold no room for lies, fantasies or mere stories.

With the banishment of fiction, historiography emerged as a rigorous, carefully monitored discipline, forever suspicious of its sources, forever sorting verifiable truths from untruths or mere conjectures. Paradoxically, however, the *form* of the historical text remained virtually indistinguishable from the literary: the realist novel had developed a disguise which blurred the difference between fact and fiction, presenting as history its fabricated illusion and so in a sense mocking history's efforts to distance itself from literature. The problem for history seems to be that however scientific its methods of verification, when it comes to telling about the past, the account will take the form of a story. In making the past tellable, the narrative form, with its beginnings and endings, its demands for coherence and intelligibility, and its tendency to account subjectively for experience, fashions that past into texts hardly distinguishable from fiction. Realising that the narrativisation of real events in itself implies some kind of distortion of, or departure from 'truth', some historians have attempted to escape narrative categories altogether. 'Quantitative history', which seeks to avoid interpretation and let the facts 'speak for themselves', is one response to the dilemma. Another is the systematic analysis of all previous accounts for the purpose of identifying the types of distortion, structural, cultural and individual, they embody.

A number of writers have in recent years pointed out that 'objectivist' history, with its prejudice against fictional forms, has chosen to overlook the function of narrative in the production of meaning. 'How else', asks Hayden White,

> can any 'past,' which is by definition comprised of events, processes, structures, and so forth that are considered to be no longer perceivable, be represented in either consciousness or discourse except in an 'imaginary' way? Is it not possible that the question of narrative in any discussion of historical theory is always finally about the function of imagination in the production of a specifically human truth? (White, 1984:33)

Language and narrative are part of the 'systems of meaning-production' shared by disciplines such as history, literature and religion. They are the means by which a culture presents the world to itself and attempts to make sense of it:

> The historical narrative does not, as narrative, dispel false beliefs about the past, human life, the nature of the community, and so on; what it does is test the capacity of a culture's fictions to endow

real events with the kinds of meaning that literature displays to consciousness through its fashioning of patterns of 'imaginary' events (ibid.:22).

The validity of a historical narrative does not, according to White's formulation, reside in its factual accuracy, but in its ability to present the past as meaningful, to *explain* the past in ways that can be perceived as satisfactory according to a culture's fictional constructions of itself.

The failure of this type of postmodern theorising to distinguish sharply between history and fiction may disturb our instinctual sense of reality. As David Lodge writes, 'history may be, in a philosophical sense, a fiction, but it does not feel like that when we miss a train or somebody starts a war' (1977:109). This 'commonsense' reaction is perfectly understandable in its concern to retain the notion of an experiential reality as the subject of meaningful human action. But brushing aside the postmodern claim as purely 'philosophical', Lodge misses the important point that fiction does not preclude action or experience: war is, perhaps more than any other human event, both a product and a generator of fictions, but its fictionality does not, unfortunately, prevent people from getting killed or countries from being ruined. Lurking behind the distrust of constructed hyperrealities lies a nostalgic longing for a lost 'authentic' reality, a reality which somehow can be reached (or in some golden past could be reached) without recourse to fictions. But reality has never *not* been hyperreal; it has always been 'constructed' in the sense that it has been validated, made intelligible, through fictional transformation. This fact does not make it less real: it is simply absurd to argue, as some have in the wake of postmodern theorising, that the real world as such has somehow ceased to exist. To acknowledge the fictionality, or provisionality, of our perception of the real is not to abdicate from any sense of responsibility. The powerful fictions of the past, and of the present, exist to be acted upon, and must be acted upon in any bid to control or transform the real.

According to Linda Hutcheon (1988, 1989), the most characteristic form of postmodern fiction is what she calls 'historiographic metafiction'. But historiographic metafiction has always existed;

there is a sense in which all historical fiction is a conscious rewriting of the past, an attempt to fill in gaps in existing knowledge, or to question received fictions as to the meaning of what happened. Historical fiction has always violated ontological boundaries, presented the real and the fictional as if they belonged to the same level of reality. Napoleon interacts with fictional characters in Tolstoy's *War and Peace*, and in *The Timeless Land* Eleanor Dark draws on historical figures such as Watkin Tench and Arthur Phillip, citing their letters and diaries, but showing them acting and thinking in accordance with a version of Australian history which would have been unthinkable at the time of the First Fleet. The difference between such fictions and the more overtly reflexive texts Hutcheon has in mind is that conventional historical fiction has a tendency to smooth over ontological contradictions, making the transition from fact to fiction discreet, hardly noticeable. Contemporary historiographic metafiction on the other hand flaunts its violation of ontological boundaries and its anachronistic treatment of the past, calling attention to itself as an imaginary construct, but by so doing questioning the validity of the versions of history we are accustomed to regard as factual.

'Historical fictions', writes Brian McHale, 'must be *realistic* fictions; a fantastic historical fiction is an anomaly' (1987:88). But in terms of the fact/fiction distinction, realistic fiction is as much of an anomaly as fantasy; there is no *natural* way of fictionalising the story of the past. By deconstructing the assumptions of the nineteenth-century historical novel, Peter Carey's *Oscar and Lucinda* highlights the paradoxes which lie at the heart of all historical fiction. Carey's novel is solidly anchored in history. It abounds in references to historical figures and events and it offers a well-documented overview of the economic, social, and intellectual climate of the mid-nineteenth century both in England and Australia. The first-person narrator scrupulously establishes his own credentials: he is the great-grandson of the protagonist Oscar Hopkins and his story, told with the hindsight of more than a hundred years, is based on family tradition as well as documentary evidence. He treats his sources critically, having learnt, he says, to distrust local history. He is particularly suspicious of his mother's proud version of her family history. But, having scrupulously established his authority, he goes on to abandon all verisimilitude in his story-telling practices. The biographer leaves behind all pretence at objectivity and instead presents an omniscient account of the past, claiming knowledge of the thoughts and feelings of his distant ancestor, commenting on the past from a position of seemingly unassailable wisdom. (In realist fiction, *Madame Bovary* offers a good example of a similar ploy.) It further transpires (but only at the end of the novel) that the family tradition on which the narrative is based is itself nothing but a fabrication: Oscar Hopkins met and married the narrator's great-grandmother on the very last day of his life. The time they had together was just enough for a furtive sexual intercourse, the signing of a few documents, and death, but not for the telling of tales. The narrator, in other words, is not recording history; he is inventing the past. But the past he invents is different from the version inherited from his mother. In contrast to what Kirsten Holst-Petersen (1991:110) calls the mother's 'imperial' story, a story of progress and civilisation, he presents a version of the colonial past in which cruelty and insensitivity is foregrounded. This story is associated with the narrator's father, and presented as a revenge on the bullying, hypocritical mother. The reader is made aware that the narrator, his parents and their motivations are themselves fictitious, but they serve to illustrate the important point which runs through the novel: history is interpretation, the past and the present are ideologically constructed according to the interests of particular individuals or groups. Working within the trappings of the conventional historical novel, Peter Carey shows us a 'history' which in terms of both form and content yields to the pressure of fiction: the realism of the story-telling turns out to be a fabrication, so do the stories of the colonial past. But the provisional nature of the past does not invalidate all histories. In terms of the moral framework of Carey's fiction, there can be little doubt which version is given the value of truth.

The purpose of much historical fiction, and metafiction, is to record the viewpoint of those who are left out of 'official' histories. In *Oscar and Lucinda* the Aboriginal perspective is offered as a corrective to white versions of history, and similar strategies are employed in much contemporary fiction from post-colonial societies (such as Toni Morrison's delving into the past of Black America and Salman Rushdie's re-creation of Indian history). Historians have in recent years shown an increasing interest in the history of marginalised groups (racial minorities, women, the poor, and so on), but the difficulty for historiography, and the advantage for fiction-writers, is that the past of such groups is often poorly documented, and so in a sense less resistant to fictional treatment. When Kate Grenville sets out to retell the history of Australia from the point of view of women, she finds that her female characters have inevitably busied themselves with mundane tasks 'while history happened elsewhere': 'There has been a Joan cooking, washing and sweeping through every event of history, although she has not been mentioned in the books until now' (Grenville, 1988:5). The real past of these women is not recorded, and so *Joan Makes History* has to be an imaginative recreation. One by one, the women emerge from the anonymity of their lives, but their shared name, Joan, underscores their lack of historical status, their existence outside the norms of historical narrative.

'Histories' such as those of Carey and Grenville are apocryphal in the sense that their versions of the past are unauthorised, but while their *interpretation* of history may be in conflict with authorised versions, they do not directly contradict the course of events. Historiographic metafiction does not always content itself with writing history in the margins of what is generally accepted as true; some texts cast aside all concern with verisimilitude, wilfully distorting chronology and falsifying evidence, sometimes even suspending the laws of nature. History becomes a version of fantastic literature, testing the real from a position well outside its conventional boundaries. Classic examples are Ishmael Reed's *Flight to Canada* in which the assassination of Abraham Lincoln is *televised*, and Carlos Fuentes' *Terra Nostra*, an alternative history of Spain. Departures from 'real' history are sometimes clearly signalled. Terry Eagleton, for example, concludes the first chapter of his novel *Saints and Scholars* by taking a break from history at the moment of James Connolly's execution after the defeat of the Easter Rising in Dublin in 1916: 'Let us arrest those bullets in mid air, prise open a space in these close-packed events through which Jimmy may scamper, blast him out of the dreary continuum of history into a different place altogether' (Eagleton, 1987:10). The 'place' to which Connolly is transported is a curious mixture of history, fiction and theory. It contains Ludwig Wittgenstein, philosopher, Nikolai Bakhtin, brother of the literary theorist Mikhail Bakhtin, Leopold Bloom, on 'loan' from Joyce's *Ulysses*, as well as a couple of other Irish characters invented for the occasion. Gathered in a cottage in Connemara, this incongruous group grapple with the question of history: is it real or is it a mere fiction? Connolly agrees that the rebellion he is engaged in is a struggle between conflicting fictions, Irish nationalism against the myth of imperialism. His concern, however, is with the power of each fiction, the military power behind it, but also the power of words. His defeat will not be total as long as his own life and death are recruited into the service of his nation's narrative of revolt. By ensuring that the struggle is kept alive, fiction exercises the power to change the course of history. Ironically, it is the doubly fictional Leopold Bloom who turns out to be the man of action. 'You might be a bleeding fiction', he says to his philosophising companions. 'You look pretty much like one to me. I happen to be real. I think I'm just about the only real person here.' (ibid.:135)

Delving deep into the terrifying magic of language and reality, the Argentine writer Luisa Valenzuela in *The Lizard's Tail* writes history as fantasy. Her story is at one level a fictionalised biography of José López Rega, Minister of Social Welfare and leader of a right-wing terrorist group; it is also an allegory of tyranny and megalomania in which figures of language engender a reality which has the quality of a hallucination. López Rega *did* practise witchcraft, and his political manoeuvrings and murderous plots were legendary, but in this book history defies reality in a manner which surpasses all rational belief. One characteristic of the sorcerer, for example, is his androgyny: he has a third testicle, which he says is his sister, Estrella. As man-woman, he claims to be capable of self-engendering, a dream of ultimate power not affected by the temporality of individual existence. The novel's other main character is a fictional version of the novelist, Valenzuela herself, who comments on her story and ponders its balance of reality and fantasy: 'A novelist is not in the world to do good but to try to know and transmit what is known; or is it to invent and transmit what is intuited?' (Valenzuela, 1987:129). Pitting the novelist's tricks against the destructive tricks of the sorcerer, she also wonders whether *writing* is the best way to respond to tyranny: 'Sitting down to write when over there, almost beside you, only a step away, innocent people are being tortured, killed, and one writes as the only possible way to counterattack. Goddamnit, what irony, what futility' (ibid.:226). Realising that she, by writing about the sorcerer, in some sense has become implicated in his evil plot, she makes the decision to put down her pen, thereby putting a stop to his story of murderous magic.

The Lizard's Tail investigates the deadly fictions of political terror at the same time as it questions the role that can be played by literary fictions in keeping them alive or destroying them. Metahistorical and metafictional concerns intersect as both history and literature are shown to depend, ultimately, on the power of stories: power to spellbind and to manipulate, power to command trust or terror, power to maintain or transform the way we view the world. Facts and fictions alike depend for their interest, credibility and authority on the power invested in the narrative act.

4

Refiguring the
Narrative Act

Writing, when properly managed, (as you may be sure I think mine is) is but a different name for conversation: As no one, who knows what he is about in good company, would venture to talk all;—so no author, who understands the just boundaries of decorum and good breeding, would presume to think all: The truest respect which you can pay to the reader's understanding, is to halve this matter amicably, and leave him something to imagine, in his turn, as well as yourself. (Sterne, 1967:127)

As Tristram Shandy argues in the most celebrated metafiction in the English language, the art of fiction should be regarded as an act of communication, an exchange between author and reader which, in the good gentleman's opinion, should be arranged democratically so as to give each partner an equal role. But in order to think of a literary text as an act of communication, or speech act, as it is called in linguistic analysis, we need to consider important differences between literary communication and other types of verbal exchange. Unlike 'normal' face-to-face conversation, litera-ture does not involve the simultaneous presence of both sender and addressee; and the context, so important to the meaning of most verbal acts, is unstable. The reader is absent from the scene of writing, thus unable to provide feedback, and at the time of reading, the author is not there to ensure that we get the 'correct' message. The author cannot truly legislate for the reception of her/his text:

we can only guess at how Shakespeare intended us to understand his work but must assume that the passing of time and the multiplication of readers have affected its intelligibility in important ways. According to Ross Chambers (1984), the constitutive feature of literary communication in western culture is precisely its deferral, its alienation from an immediate communicational situation. The move from oral to written story-telling complicates the relationship between sender and receiver, rendering both these agents and the messages that pass between them indeterminate.

Julian Barnes offers a witty reminder of this point in his novel *Flaubert's Parrot* (1984). An elderly English widower makes several visits to the native country of Gustave Flaubert around the French city of Rouen, searching for biographical clues to the work of the great writer. At a museum in Rouen his attention is caught by a stuffed parrot, claimed to be the very parrot Flaubert immortalised as Loulou in his tale 'A Simple Heart'. Documentary evidence confirms that Flaubert borrowed the parrot from the museum and placed it on his work-table as an inspiration for the creation of Loulou. The Englishman, whose name is Geoffrey Braithwaite, feels strangely moved by the parrot, and through it even experiences a kind of communion with the long-dead writer. To him, the parrot comes to stand for Flaubert himself; the preserved bird becomes a guarantee of the authorial presence, somehow putting the reader in touch with the origin, the true meaning of Flaubert's work. It turns out, however, that there is more than one parrot. On his visit to another collection of Flaubert memorabilia at the writer's summer pavilion in Croisset, Braithwaite comes across another parrot, also claimed to be the authentic Loulou. Intrigued by the conflicting claims, obsessed by the need to know which of the parrots is truly Flaubert's, he begins an extensive research. After letters to various academics and authorities, a close examination of the two birds and of Flaubert's text, he finally, after two years, pays a visit to the oldest member of the 'Society of the Friends of Flaubert'. Here he learns that the museum from which Flaubert borrowed his bird had not one but *fifty* parrots, any one of which could have been the one the author borrowed. The novel concludes with the Englishman in the museum's reserve collection, staring at a room full of birds. The original bird, like the original meaning of Flaubert's text, disappears under the dust of history, and the multitude of surviving specimens can only, parrot-like, mime the presence of the lost origin. Braithwaite's Flaubert, moreover, is a product of destination (the reader) as well as origin (the author): the Englishman is motivated in his obsessive search by connections between himself and the writer. Like Flaubert's Madame Bovary, his wife has been unfaithful; like Madame Bovary, she has committed suicide by taking poison. Braithwaite's attempt to make sense of literature is in the end revealed as an effort to make sense of his own life.

The literary text, untethered from its origin and forever resituating its destination, has in a number of critical discourses become the very model for the context-free, self-sufficient artefact. New Criticism, structuralism and post-structuralism alike have directed attention away from readers and writers to focus on the text itself, its internal structures, its capacity to escape determinate sense-making systems. But these discourses have been challenged by other, more 'pragmatic' schools of literary theory, which criticise them for ignoring questions of agency and meaning, as well as the impact of the text's various contexts on its creation and reception. In the name of 'common sense' M. H. Abrams, for example, deplores Derrida's apparent disregard for anything but textual free play:

> Derrida's chamber of texts is a sealed echo-chamber in which meanings are reduced to a ceaseless echolalia, a vertical and lateral reverberation from sign to sign of ghostly non-presences emanating from no voice, intended by no one, referring to nothing, bombinating in a void. (Abrams, 1972:431)

Against the obvious fact that literary texts cannot function as direct communication stands the equally obvious fact that communication *does* occur, however displaced, deferred, or otherwise complicated by textual and contextual factors. Narrative theory, reader-response criticism, political criticism and speech-act theory are among the many approaches seeking to define the kinds of exchange taking place in literature and examine its various contexts: those created by texts themselves and those within which literary texts are inscribed. Against the notion of literature as a context-free linguistic performance stands the view, voiced by Mary Louise Pratt, that '*literature is a context, too*, not the absence of one' (1977:99).

In the study of literature as communication a new function for fictional reflexivity emerges. Literary texts are not content to function as 'sealed echo-chambers', resounding in a void to which no authors or readers can gain access. On the contrary, they compensate for their alienated status by creating the conditions for their own reception. The text has the power 'to control its own impact through the act of situational self-definition' (Chambers, 1984:24), and thus in a sense limit the range of meanings available to the reader. Theorising about the act of story-telling from within story-telling itself, the reflexive text stages its various agents (authors, readers, narrators, narratees, characters) in order to instruct real readers, telling them something about the roles, powers and duties which are theirs in the curious conversational practice we call literature.

Enter the actors

At the beginning of Luigi Pirandello's play *Six Characters in Search of an Author* a play rehearsal is interrupted by six people of rather problematic status: they are characters in a play that has not yet been written. They are not simply actors out of work, but 'real' characters, whose tragic lives, they insist, deserve to be recorded and acted out, if only they could find an author to take them in charge. The paradox of their situation is of course that there must be an author for them to exist at all; if there is no author, there can be no characters. The absence of the author is only apparent: Pirandello, the precondition for the existence of the play and so in a sense its most important character, has been there all the time.

Like the absent author in Pirandello's play, all actors in the drama performed by literary texts tend to be elusive, difficult to locate and even more difficult to define. Readers are at once in the text and outside it, unable to change the text but responsible for its realisation. Fictional characters, on the other hand, figure in the text but have no material existence outside it; their *reality*, however convincing, depends on the extra-textual activities of authors and readers. In order to describe more precisely the function of the various agents in the literary act, narrative theory has thrown up a vast support cast of narrators and narratees, implied authors and implied readers, focalisers and model readers (to name a few), whose roles are vigorously debated. It has also been observed that literary communication occurs simultaneously at several levels. The author–reader, or, as some theorists prefer, text–reader relationship is mediated through speech acts performed by other agents: the voice that 'speaks' in the text is not that of the author but that of the narrator, who communicates directly with the narratee and only indirectly with the reader. Moreover, the narrator–narratee speech act may be relayed through a a number of other channels of communication, with fictional characters performing the roles of internal narrators and narratees. To further complicate the 'communi-cation model' for fiction, it has been observed that the functions of reading and writing are distributed among several agents, and that each agent may, in the course of the story, perform several functions:

> The author is not the only source of meaning, nor is the reader the only interpreter . . . The characters usually 'read' and interpret the events in which they are involved. The fact that critics often argue about whether a character has interpreted his or her world correctly serves as evidence that interpretations exist *within* a story as well as in what readers say about it. Narrators are also readers and interpreters. And finally, the writer is a reader and interpreter, just as the real reader, by posing and answering questions, becomes a writer or rewriter of the story. In other words, the entire communication model exists with each of its discrete parts. (Martin, 1986:169, here paraphrasing Miller, 1982)

Deferred, multiple, unstable and indeterminate—the literary speech act is of a complexity which defies normal linguistic analysis, and many linguists and critics therefore conclude that all communica-tion models for literary texts must be seen as inadequate. But it is precisely the complexity of literary communication that fascinates reflexive fiction, which has always known that authors, readers and contexts are central to the literary experience. Metafiction marvels in the theoretical difficulties which have literary analysts in despair, and gleefully juggles the roles of author, reader and character to the confusion but also to the delight of their real readers. And not infrequently, such reflexive playfulness makes sound theoretical sense.

Roland Barthes' programmatic essay 'The Death of the Author' (in Barthes, 1977:142–8) presents a timely warning against both the tendency to regard the literary text as a direct expression of the author's personal vision and the practice of limiting the text's potential for meaning in the name of an extra-textual authority. But Barthes' words can never be taken literally as long as the function of literature in our culture remains linked to the name of the author and the authority it invokes. A. S. Byatt exposes the ambivalence in our attitude towards authors in her novel *Possession*, where a number of literary scholars pursue the lost manuscripts of two Victorian poets, partly with a view to rectifying literary history, partly also because they are aware of the value (material as well as professional) such documents hold for them. The long-dead authors are literally disturbed in their graves, robbed of their intimate secrets, and in the light of newly discovered facts about their lives, their poems become recontextualised, read as acts of communication rather than free-standing texts. Staring at the death-mask of the famous poet, the novel's hero, ironically named Roland, reflects on the complex mode of existence the author has acquired for him:

> He thought about the death mask. He could and could not say that the mask and the man were dead. What had happened to him was that the ways in which it *could* be said had become more interesting than the idea that it could not. (Byatt, 1990:473)

If it can be said that the author, mask, man (or woman), is dead, it must also be said that the function of the author is central to the discursive practice called literature. Michel Foucault (1977) has pointed to the author's legal function as the holder of property rights over written texts, and argued that the name of the author constitutes a principle of unity governing the way we talk about literature. Moreover, as Susan Sniader Lanser (1981) argues, the author represents a special kind of formalised power in our society: the processes of selection and publication endow the literary text with an authority not granted other verbal acts. The reader comes to the literary text with certain expectations, willing to lend it a special kind of attention. The focus for the cultural status enjoyed by literature is the name of the author. The author, according to this construction, is not so much an individual as a cultural function.

The problem for both authors and readers arises from the fact that authors, in addition to being names and functions, *are* individuals too, and their various roles are not always compatible. The best illustration of this dilemma is undoubtedly Jorge Luis Borges's short parable 'Borges and I' (1970:282–3), which explores the transformation of the literary text: starting as the personal vision of an author, it becomes the property of language and tradition. Metafiction, written by *real* authors interested in literary theory, not surprisingly takes the paradoxical function of the author as one of its favourite themes. 'What is strange and disorienting about the postmodernist author', writes Brian McHale, 'is that even when s/he appears to know that s/he is only a function, s/he chooses to behave, if only sporadically, like a subject, a presence' (1987:201). In *The French Lieutenant's Woman*, for example, a character who both is and is not the 'real' John Fowles enters the world of the fictional characters to discuss the role of the author and to demonstrate his authority over the fate of the protagonists. In Italo Calvino's *If On a Winter's Night a Traveller*, where most of the characters are either readers or writers (or both), the distinction between author-as-function and author-as-individual causes some embarrassment and much hilarity. The character Cavedagna works for a publishing firm and spends his day dealing with real and would-be authors, but dreams of distant childhood days when he would hide in the chicken coop to communicate with authors who were nothing but names on the tattered covers of cheap editions:

> he deals with them every day, he knows their fixations, indecisions, susceptibilities, egocentricities, and yet the true authors remain those who for him were only a name on a jacket, a word that was part of the title, authors who had the same reality as their characters, as the places mentioned in the books, who existed and didn't exist at the same time, like those characters and those countries. The author was an invisible point from which the books came, a void traveled by ghosts, an underground tunnel that put other worlds in communication with the chicken coop of his boyhood. (Calvino, 1992:101–2)

Ludmilla, the 'Other Reader' and the main female character in the novel, is like Cavedagna uninterested in real authors. As her sister Lotaria explains, 'Ludmilla insists it's better not to know authors personally, because the real person never corresponds to the image you form of him from reading his books' (ibid.:185–6). When the author Silas Flannery, whose books she loves, falls in love with *her*, she refuses his advances: 'It would have nothing to do with the author Silas Flannery whose novels I read . . . As I was explaining to you, you are two separate persons, whose relationships cannot interact' (ibid.:190). Flannery's jealousy is all the more keen as he realises that his rival is none other than his own 'second self', who exists only as black marks on a page and in Ludmilla's imagination.

As reader, Ludmilla is both an individual and a function of the novels she reads. Her absorption, her eagerness to find out what happens next, makes her the ideal reader of the kind of books Flannery writes; in her personal relationships as a woman she is less easily taken in. To Calvino's reader, she is, of course, also a character of fiction, another kind of textual function. *If On a Winter's Night . . .* thus illustrates the various roles narrative theory has defined for the reader. The function of the reader *in* the text has been theorised by critics such as Wolfgang Iser (1974) and Umberto Eco (1979) in terms of 'implied', 'ideal', or 'model' readers, but, as has been pointed out, these textual readers are themselves constructed by *real* readers (in most cases by critics); the reading positions offered by the text and the interpretative positions occupied by readers are at least as complex as those occupied by the senders of the literary message. 'One thing is clear', writes Marie Maclean, 'that the idea of the reader as a competent, serene, intelligent, and objective receiver of messages is just as much a myth as that of authorial "intention" regarded as a single conscious act of sending a message' (1988:33).

There are many ways for readers and the acts of reading and interpretation to be dramatised in a literary text. Direct reader address is one of them: the narrator takes a pause from story-telling to appeal to an extra-textual 'Dear Madam', 'Sir', or simply 'you', offering advice or admonition, pleading for sympathy or rebuffing criticism. The problem is that this kind of communication is necessarily one-sided: the extra-textual reader is simply not there to answer back, and conducting a conversation in this manner can be rather frustrating. Narrators solve the problem in various ways, generally by hypothesising about the reader, imagining a particular kind of reader or a particular response. Tristram Shandy thus variously addresses male and female readers, sympathetic and hostile ones. Calvino creates two readers, also male and female. Interestingly, though, his direct address is almost exclusively directed at the male reader.

The reader's contribution to the literary speech act, according to Wolfgang Iser (1978), consists in filling in the 'gaps' in the text, supplying the information not furnished by the narrator. A great deal of critical debate has surrounded the nature of these gaps or indeterminacies: is it possible to say which parts of the text are determinate and which indeterminate, and who is to decide—the real reader or a reader construct created by the text (see, for example, Fish, 1981; Iser, 1981). Metafiction frequently plays with the idea of literalising the reader's input. A good example is Raymond Federman's *Take It or Leave It*, which includes a question-naire the reader is supposed to fill in and return to the author, who in turn will take it into account when composing the remainder of the text. In *If On a Winter's Night* . . . Calvino's fictionalised reader comes across a text in which blank pages and printed pages alternate, an idea borrowed from *Tristram Shandy* and a literal illustration of Shandy's ideal of equal contributions by author and reader.

The impossibility of incorporating the actual reader's response, ironically vindicated by metafiction's playful attempts at doing so, necessitates the construction of more accessible, fictional readers. The second-person pronoun 'you' almost inevitably drifts towards the function of the third-person pronoun as it ceases to address the reader and instead comes to stand for a fictional character. Calvino's 'you' initially addresses everyone who has opened the book, but after only a few pages the reader is a particular reader, who becomes the protagonist of a novel about reading. Overtly reflexive texts such as *If On a Winter's Night* . . . call attention to a practice common to all fiction: by staging characters engaged in acts of reading and interpreting, literary texts are able to theorise about such activities and by so doing attempt to produce the conditions for their own reception.

Dramatised readers thinking about, discussing and performing acts of reading, like those we encounter in *If On a Winter's Night* . . . , or in novels such as A. S. Byatt's *Possession* or Julian Barnes's

Flaubert's Parrot, embody the reader function in particularly
obvious ways. Through these readers, real readers are presented
with a running commentary on the nature of the text–reader (or
author–reader) relationship: motivations for reading, attitudes and
expectations fostered by other texts and other authors, enchant-
ment or critical detachment, and so on. Other fictions display their
preoccupation with reading indirectly, often by means of embedded story-telling acts or other examples of readerly *mise en abyme.*
In David Lodge's novel *Small World* (which the author labels a
romance), the character Morris Zapp listens to Phillip Swallow
telling the story of his romantic adventure with Joy. Zapp's reaction
changes from the initial detachment of the professional critic to
complete involvement in the emotional impact of the plot. When
Small World later takes up the same story, staging another encounter between Phillip and his lost love, the reader in a sense feels
authorised to model his or her reaction on that of its first audience.

The *mise en abyme* of reading does not necessarily involve
stories or texts: any object or situation which requires interpretation
can be made to stand for an act of reading. The figure in the carpet
in Henry James's story of that name offers an apt example: as the
characters puzzle over the meaning of the figure, so the reader
puzzles over the meaning of James's 'Figure . . . ' In yet other texts,
certain plot structures reflect the role of the reader. The detective
story, in particular, presents the investigator in a search for
knowledge similar to that instigated by the literary text, where the
reader has to sift through textual clues in a search for meaning. The
popularity of this genre in contemporary metafiction is undoubtedly
related to its reflexive potential. A good example is Marguerite
Duras' novel *L'Amante anglaise,* which rewrites the detective genre
reflexively, explicitly relating the acts of reading and investigation,
but frustrating the reader as well as the detective's desire for a
solution to the enigma.

How, we may wonder, is the reader to know whether a model
for the text–reader relationship is indeed offered as a *mise en
abyme* of the reading prescribed for the text in which it occurs?
Could it not on the contrary be regarded as an anti-model,
illustrating a mode of reception discredited by the text and
instructing the reader to read otherwise? There can obviously be no

easy answer to such questions. Just as the real reader is free to accept or reject textual instructions on its own reception, so the text is able to offer conflicting instructions, models as well as anti-models for its desired relationship with the reader. The 'ideal reading situation', as defined by the text, is, just like the 'ideal reader', a concept which owes its existence to a prior act of interpretation. When reading models and anti-models multiply, readers may legitimately disagree about what instructions have been issued. In the case of complex reflexive texts the question is, moreover, complicated by the fact that a great number of reading positions may be offered as not only possible, but equally valid or, as the case may be, invalid. Remembering Braithwaite's dilemma in *Flaubert's Parrot*, we could say that there are simply too many parrots to choose from.

Mark Henshaw's novel *Out of the Line of Fire* which, as pointed out earlier, opens with an intertextual reference to *If On a Winter's Night . . .* , stages the acts of reading, writing, and interpretation in a manner which defies any attempt to locate source and destination precisely. The novel reads like a kind of metafictional whodunit: who has written what, or whom, what positions are offered authors and readers, what kind of status (fact, fiction) can be claimed for characters and events? Initially about an author in search of a character, it turns out to have been, all along, about a character in search of an author. When the first-person narrator becomes interested in Wolfi, he sees him as a character in a projected novel. Wolfi later disappears, leaving the narrator a pile of documents related to his life with the instructions 'Perhaps *you* can make something of this' (Henshaw, 1988:49). The narrator and would-be author thus becomes a reader, sifting through the material in his effort to solve the riddle of his lost friend. Unsuccessful, he eventually seeks the assistance of a more perceptive reader, Wolfi's sister, who alerts him to the clues he has failed to recognise. He finally realises that his quest has been stage-managed by Wolfi himself: the real author is dead, but posthumously asserts his authority over the text of his life by directing the reader's search. When the hapless reader and detective himself turns author, writing the story of his own search for Wolfi, he has somehow to duplicate Wolfi's authority, create a position for *his* reader which will incorporate both bewilderment and guided search for meaning.

In *Out of the Line of Fire*, as in many other reflexive fictions, the roles of author, character, and reader become provisional positions, constantly renegotiated between the principal actors in the metafictional drama. Their relationship is unstable, as is the authority each of them exerts over the narrative in which he/she figures. Like most human relations, literary communication mediates a precarious balance of power: power to narrate, power to interpret, power, finally, to accept or decline the roles offered by one's partners in the literary act.

Authors versus readers: sexual/textual intercourse

I am writing in . . . a convention universally accepted at the time of my story: that the novelist stands next to God. He may not know all, yet he tries to pretend that he does. But I live in the age of Alain Robbe-Grillet and Roland Barthes; if this is a novel, it cannot be a novel in the modern sense of the word. (Fowles, 1970:85)

When the narrator of *The French Lieutenant's Woman* interrupts the story to speculate about his own role in it, he notes an important change that has occurred between the time of his story (1867) and the time of the telling (1967): the author is no longer in a position of absolute authority over his or her creation. 'In the new theological image, with freedom our first principle, not authority' (ibid.:86), he continues, authors can no longer be omniscient, but have to respect the rights of the other players in the fictional game: characters and readers. No less pompous for his partial abdication, he goes on to change the rules of his fiction, ordering the characters to choose their own destiny, giving the reader a choice of endings. The newfound 'freedom', however, comes with its own set of prescriptions defining the roles of readers and characters in the new narrative order. It could be argued that the benevolent democracy of 'the age of Alain Robbe-Grillet and Roland Barthes' masks another bid for authorial power: the rhetoric of freedom becomes the means by which the playful author-figure of postmodern fiction enlists readerly cooperation in a new and not necessarily less dictatorial regime.

Both fiction and literary theory have in recent years tended to present the text as, in Marie Maclean's terms, 'a strategic battleground' (1988:15) between narrator and narratee, or between author and reader. The author, generally portrayed as an authoritarian figure limiting the text's potential for meaning, is challenged by representatives of reader power and forced to give ground. In Roland Barthes' formulation ('the birth of the reader must be at the cost of the death of the Author' (1977:148)) it is a battle to the death, the demise of the author signalling the birth of the reader as the sole arbiter of meaning. The battle is in the final count between conflicting ideologies of reading. Often, as in this passage by Robert Crosman, it is presented in liberationist terms:

> The convention that authors make meaning arose from a desire to think of truth as single and unequivocal, and is part of an ideology of society that is authoritarian and hierarchical. It is true—to the extent that it is true—as all conventions are: by the consent of the members of that society. My impression is that this consent is being withdrawn today at an accelerating rate, as people perceive that freedom is not incompatible with order, and that order is not necessarily hierarchical. (Crosman, 1980:163–4)

When discussing readerly freedom, many critics posit an opposition between the closed, authoritarian (most often realist) text of conventional fiction and the open, reader-friendly text of contemporary, innovative modes such as reflexivity. Barthes (1975a, 1975b, 1977) sets up several such oppositions: the conventional text is the readerly text, the *texte de plaisir* or the work, by contrast to the writerly text, the *texte de jouissance* or, simply, the text. In the writerly text, the reader is the creator, not so much of meaning as of the text itself, whose potential for meaning is infinite and irreducible.

Contemporary metafiction, frustrating conventional expectations and thereby calling attention to the reader's role in the construction of the fictional universe, is often cited as a model for the freedom-inducing text. This is how Linda Hutcheon describes the process in *Narcissistic Narrative*:

> The unsettled reader is forced to scrutinize his concepts of art as well as his life values. Often he must revise his understanding of

what he reads so frequently that he comes to question the very possibility of understanding. In doing so he might be freed from enslavement not only to the empirical, but also to his own set patterns of thought and imagination. (Hucheon, 1984:150)

The freedom Hutcheon has in mind, however, differs from Barthes' ideal of irreducible plurality and consists in a very particular kind of reprogramming. The reader has no real choice—he or she is 'forced' on the road to liberation: 'He is assaulted, frustrated in his normal novelistic expectations. The author seems to want to change the nature of literature by altering the nature of the reader's participation in it' (ibid.:150). Metafiction which thematises the role of the reader is here shown to have a didactic purpose: the reader must be taught how to read differently. Freedom, as Hutcheon points out, implies responsibility, and the responsibility of the 'free' reader ironically turns out to be that of reading the text as it wants to be read.

The French Lieutenant's Woman offers two versions of the last chapter. One is a happy ending, the other an inconclusive one. The inconclusive ending comes last, an indication, perhaps, that this is the *real* ending. But there are even stronger reasons to suspect that the reader has no real choice in the matter of endings. The first version of the last chapter allows the reader, temporarily, to indulge in a bit of wishful thinking, but the reader who has read the novel carefully will know that he or she must choose the final ending or fail the test of freedom. Freedom in the sense of liberation from conventional expectations (a kind of freedom advocated throughout the book) ironically annihilates the reader's freedom of choice.

In the name of reader-power some texts invent ways of constructing the story which escape the rigid linearity of the traditional book. B. S. Johnson's *The Unfortunates* consists of twenty-seven unnumbered sections which come loose in a box: readers are invited to arrange them in any order they please, and so construct their own storyline. The format aptly illustrates the idea of randomness, which is a central thematic concern in the text. In terms of the chronology of the story, however, the order in which the sections are read matters not in the slightest. The order of events can easily be reconstructed from the sections, and so the randomness, and the reader's contribution, in the end have little impact on its meaning.

The game structure—with its implications of randomness—is a recurrent feature of metafiction. The dice, however, turns out to be loaded: the activity of the reader is channelled according to rules determined by the text. Linda Hutcheon herself came to realise that her earlier notion of readerly freedom could be misleading. In *A Theory of Parody* she writes: 'Being made to feel that we are actively participating in the generation of meaning is no guarantee of freedom; manipulators who make us feel in control are no less present for all their careful concealment' (Hutcheon, 1985:183). Similarly, Umberto Eco, who earlier (1979) theorised what he called the 'open' text in terms of readerly freedom, has more recently stressed the limits of the reader's contribution and vindicated the rights of the text to restrict the field of interpretation (Eco, 1990). The 'era of the reader' in literary theory is perhaps, then, nearing its end, but the battle for supremacy over the literary text is by no means over.

Indeed, one could argue that the narrative act itself depends for its survival on the continuation of the battle: if either opponent, victorious or defeated, leaves the battlefield, literary interaction must cease. Authors and readers are therefore partners more than they are enemies, their strategies involving moves which will ensure cooperation as well as contest. Authors can never allow themselves to forget that readers possess the supreme power, which is that of abandoning the text. The author must exercise textual authority in such a way as to ensure that this will not happen. Not surprisingly, then, textual communication is frequently represented as an act of love: the text must offer itself as an object of desire, seduce the reader, play and be played upon like the body of a lover. The apparently incompatible metaphors of sex and battle turn out to rely on the same kinds of tactic. In love and war, control of the field means ability to maintain the initiative, predict the moves of one's opponent and by so doing command the position from which he or she will view the intercourse.

Noting the constancy with which literary texts theorise their impact through the metaphor of seduction, Ross Chambers comments on the range of tactics available to them:

> Narrative seduction, then, seems as complex and varied in its tactics as are the erotic seductions of everyday life; and its range, from active enterprise, through the 'simple' invitation, to a

carefully calculated 'refusal', is not dissimilar to what can be observed wherever people relate sexually to one another. (Chambers, 1984:217)

In order to understand the dynamics of the narrative act, we need to analyse the libidinal input of readers as well as authors. One project for narrative theory, Marie Maclean suggests, could be the elaboration of a 'sex manual' for textual intercourse: 'Perhaps we need a Masters and Johnson, or even a Krafft-Ebing, of teller–hearer relationships' (1988:35). The seductive power initially granted the text by its status as literature or the prestige of its author has to be maintained by other means. Plots are structured to keep the reader's interest alive: we keep on reading in order to find out what happens next, to discover the secrets underlying the fictional intrigue. But even satisfying the reader's curiosity is not enough to ensure the continued authority of the text. In order to maintain its seductive power, perhaps to kindle the desire to *reread*, the text must have at its disposal other charms and other tactics. The text may flatter the reader or otherwise allow him or her to take a narcissistic delight in the intercourse. It may, on the other hand, go about its seductive business indirectly, denying one kind of seductive programme in order to pursue a different one. It may even, Maclean notes, play on repressed desires in the reader such as masochism or sadism. The metafictional habit of insulting the reader can thus be understood as both a reorientation of the reader and a (perverse) way of enlisting her or his libidinal cooperation. 'You, dogged, uninsultable, printoriented bastard, it's you I'm addressing, who else, from inside this monstrous fiction', thunders John Barth's narrator in *Lost in the Funhouse* (1969:123), and the uninsultable bastard goes on reading, her/his interest or libido stimulated by the ostensible show of aggression. Brian McHale observes that offending the audience may in fact count as a manifestation of love or a seductive strategy, a '"lover's quarrel" deliberately staged as the prelude to a tender reconciliation' (1987:226).

Hostility and love-making between partners in the textual intercourse become the focus for the reflexive plot in John Fowles's *Mantissa*, which, like a number of other metafictions, literalises the textual/sexual analogy and stages the narrative act as the product of sexual intercourse and sexual warfare. The partners, Miles and

Erato, occupy various roles. Miles is cast as the author, Erato as his muse, and their sexual union results in the birth of 'a lovely little story' (Fowles, 1982:48). In other versions of the plot, Erato becomes a character or a reader, and occasionally Miles appears as character in, or reader of, fictions created by Erato. Their interaction, although overtly sexual, is rarely harmonious. The proverbial battle between the sexes becomes a battle for authority over the text, a type of authority which is forever precarious and unstable. As soon as one of them feels in control, the power-base will be snatched from under his/her feet; as soon as one partner appears to be yielding ground, it turns out to have been a strategic move to gain advantage. The battle is never finally won or lost—cannot be, of course, as long as literary communication continues.

The writers and readers in *Mantissa* are parodic figures, ostensibly fictional and so clearly not to be identified with the *real* author or *real* readers of the book. The setting is also palpably unreal, variously represented as a padded cell in a mental hospital or the inside of the writer's skull. Hence the relevance of its rather claustrophobic spectacle for the *real* experience of reading may seem slight. The reflexive machinery does not, however, operate at the level of the fictional characters only. Erato and Miles constantly remind each other that there is a world outside their intercourse. Indeed, at one stage, the walls of their room are made transparent, and we become aware of a number of spectators looking in on the scene. *Mantissa* knows only too well that it is playing to a real audience, and its point, for the reader, is that the strategies of love and war thematised in the Miles–Erato relationship are duplicated in *Mantissa's* bid to capture his/her attention. As the lovers fight, make up and attempt to trap each other by verbal subterfuge and bodily ministrations, so *Mantissa* variously seduces, attacks and manipulates the reader. The battle for the text must go on, but *Mantissa*, presenting itself as the ultimate metafiction, is aware that its tactics are risky: the exasperated reader may decide that the only way to save his/her skin—or sanity—is to leave the battlefield. Balancing on the very edge of acceptable text–reader relations, metafictions like this one should perhaps come with its own health warning: reflexivity could damage the viability of the fictional contract.

Engendering the reflexive reader

According to the sexual metaphor exploited in *Mantissa* and other reflexive fictions, the text is engendered through the union ('textual intercourse') of author and muse, or author and reader. The metaphor, as John Fowles clearly demonstrates, is an infinitely flexible one, and it is also possible to twist it in such a way that the *reader* becomes the offspring, engendered by the text interacting with a number of contextual factors. One such factor is the genre to which the text is perceived to belong. The generic expectations raised by 'metafiction' as a distinct class of texts conditions the reader's reception of the individual text, which, in turn, will modify her or his perception of the genre. The processes of fictional generation are both promiscuous and circular: authors couple with readers or muses to produce texts; texts combine with genres and other framing devices to create authors and readers; readers interact with other readers to rewrite literary genres; the new genre resituates the text, thereby creating it anew, and so it goes on.

In order to locate the reader of metafiction, we need to examine not only the speech act represented by a particular text, but also the various other speech acts in which it is embedded. 'The illocutionary acts undertaken within the fiction', writes Susan Sniader Lanser, 'are framed by a more basic speech act which is the act of novelistic communication itself' (1981:292). The rules which apply to novelistic communication are distinct from those which apply to other speech acts. The 'essence of literariness or poeticality', according to Mary Louise Pratt, resides in 'a particular disposition of speaker and audience with regard to the message' (1977:87). The 'audience' of a literary text is (normally) a voluntary one, which gives up its own 'right to the floor' for the time of the textual performance, but which by so doing earns the right to pass judgement on it. The text's authority to speak is initially gained through cultural processes which confer an elevated status ('Literature') on it. Before picking up a book, a reader generally knows something about the author, and often he or she has been influenced by the reaction of former readers (critics, reviewers, cover blurbs, recommendations by friends, etc.). Controversy as well as praise may stir the reader's interest: nothing is more seductive than the text one has been warned against or forbidden. The readership of Salman Rushdie's *The Satanic Verses* was no doubt much enlarged by the fact that the book was banned and its author condemned to death. In order to describe the literary speech act, Pratt borrows from the linguistic analysis of H. P. Grice the concept of CP (the cooperative principle), which defines the attitude of speaker and hearer and the relationship between the two as determined by the particular kind of speech act in which they are engaged. Literature, she claims, is characterised by a 'hyperprotected' CP, which means that the reader is disposed (at least initially) to recognise the authority of the text and to tolerate much greater deviance from rules (linguistic, social, generic) than would be the case in most other speech acts. The reader's entry into the literary act implies a willingness to engage in the textual game, to play the roles prescribed by the text and to give it a 'fair go'. This tolerance obviously has its limits: if the text transgresses beyond a certain point, the reader may withdraw his or her consent, adopt a hostile attitude or, more drastically, close the book. At the end of the 'contract', moreover, the text becomes accountable for the reader's willing suspension of distrust: it must be perceived to have been 'worth it', to have lived up to the reader's expectations.

Metafiction selects its audience in various ways, and by classifying a text as a metafiction, readers (or critics, or publishers) activate a particular set of generic expectations which will determine its interpretation. Contemporary metafiction is generally included in the category 'postmodernist fiction', a category that carries a great many (sometimes conflicting) connotations, some of which are playfulness, difficulty and transgression. The intellectual sophistication and formal innovation associated with postmodernism has made it both fashionable and controversial; extremely popular with certain audiences, much maligned by others. Metafiction's frequent and explicit allusions to other texts and to literary theory have the same effect of dividing the readership into those who recognise the allusions and enjoy them, and those who find them tiresome either because they are unfamiliar with such matters or because they think they smack of intellectual posturing. The 'serious modern writer' in *Mantissa* is in no doubt about the audience for metafiction:

academic readers, he argues, 'are the only ones who count nowadays' (Fowles, 1982:119).

If it is true that the metafictional speech act presupposes an academic audience, or at least an audience trained to recognise intertextual allusion, it is also true that a number of individual texts single such readers out for particularly rough treatment. In *Mantissa* the modern author and his sophisticated audience are accused of betraying the art of fiction and hastening the death of the novel. *Flaubert's Parrot* quotes Flaubert's violent outbursts against the critical profession in order to mock its own critics and commentators. Lotaria, the academic reader in *If On a Winter's Night . . .*, is, unlike her sister Ludmilla, unable to interact with the text; her arid academic analysis can only bring out what *she* wants to find, not what the book has to offer. David Lodge's *Small World* stages a theory-ridden academic wasteland, finally redeemed through the agency of a naive reader, the only true lover of literature (and women).

Insulting the academic critic is not an activity exclusive to metafiction; the 'ivory tower' of the academy has always been an easy target for popular wit. In the case of metafiction, however, it becomes a special case of the love-and-hate topos which so often characterises text–reader relationships. Some critics take this hostility at face value: it is, they argue, symptomatic of a breakdown in communication between text and reader and thus an indictment of artistic and cultural relations in the postmodern world. Charles Newman, for example, claims that American postmodern fiction, by evoking the audience as cultural enemy, 'represents an act of ultimate aggression against the contemporary audience' (1985:92). But it is also possible, as I have suggested, to interpret acts of aggression as tactical moves in a game of seduction, manoeuvres aimed at courting the reader to secure her or his cooperation. It may be that academic audiences are particularly disposed to take masochistic pleasure in being reviled, but it can also be argued that academics and other experienced readers realise that the hostility is more mimed than real: it takes place within a verbal act which protects the CP and so ensures readerly cooperation. Mary Louise Pratt likens aggression towards the reader, or other examples of what she calls *verbal jeopardy*, to the way in which words of abuse used among intimates invert their function and will be received as terms of endearment or compliments: 'As long as we are assured that the flouting interpretation will prevail, jeopardizing the CP has the effect of reinforcing intimacy' (1977:217).

Readers are never passive bystanders observing the textual spectacle from a safe distance, but unlike the reader of 'illusionist' fiction, the metafictional reader is provoked into an awareness of the role s/he plays in activating the text. By theorising and problematising the reader's function, metafiction produces readers at once aware of their participation in the fictional game and somewhat confused about what is expected of them. The text invites intimacy by staging the literary act as a collaborative project and flatters the reader by assuming that he or she will 'get' intertextual allusions. By deliberately transgressing conventional patterns of text–reader relationships, the text involves the reader in a kind or conspiratorial pact which sets itself apart from normal, run-of-the-mill fictional contracts. But the very difficulty involved in negotiating new roles may also produce a sense of alienation in the reader, a feeling reinforced by the fact that these roles frequently involve conflict and logical contradiction. Playing on the edge of intelligibility, the reader experiences the possibility of a breakdown in communication. Ross Chambers (1982:92) describes the position of the reader in such texts as situated somewhere between game and anxiety, producing a kind of 'voluptuous vertigo'. The sense of danger is, however, accompanied by the margin of security represented by the literary act itself: knowing that it is 'only a text', the reader can allow him- or herself to take pleasure in being put at risk. Metafiction thus involves the reader in a kind of catharsis, an acting out and purging of violent emotions, not, as in tragedy, through identification with the characters, but through the very performance of the role of reader.

In order to be metafictionally engendered according to the model suggested here, readers must be both *aware* of the roles they are expected to play and *willing* to accept them. If these conditions are not met, the effect of reflexivity on the reader can be a very different one. The fact that the effect so often *is* different is a clear indication, I think, that the phenomenon of fictional reflexivity and the genre metafiction remain problematic concepts for many readers and critics. One problem resides in the calculated risk built into the metafictional contract itself: many readers will respond with hostility to textual aggression and refuse to be wooed by complex strategies of seduction. Such readers simply decline the role offered them by the text and go on to read it according to different modes of reception. But what of the reader who remains largely unaware of the reflexive enterprise and his and her participation in it? What happens when reflexivity intrudes into other types of reading contracts, such as that of 'illusionist' fiction? Do readers receive the intrusive narrators in George Eliot or Thackeray, or the reflexive moments in popular authors such as Stephen King or San Antonio, as they do postmodern metafiction? My (still incomplete) answer to such questions would start with the suggestion that fictional reflexivity is a more varied and multiply coded phenomenon than what is generally accepted. The 'encoding' or 'engendering' of the reflexive reader may be as much a product of the contexts, or 'frames', surrounding the narrative act as of the nature of the act itself. I have come to suspect, moreover, that the *genre* 'metafiction' and the contexts evoked by its production are quite distinct from the phenomenon of fictional reflexivity in itself. Perhaps it is the genre, and *its* engendering, that should emerge as the main object of our critical enquiry?

5

Poetics and Politics

> Since . . . it is readily admitted, even by our conservatives, that the great contemporary artists, writers or painters, generally belong (or have belonged in the period of their most important works) to the parties of the Left, we indulge ourselves by constructing this idyllic schema: Art and Revolution advancing hand in hand, struggling for the same cause, passing through the same ordeals, facing the same dangers, gradually achieving the same conquests, acceding finally to the same apotheosis.
>
> Unfortunately, once we turn to the realm of practice, things do not turn out so well. (Robbe-Grillet, 1965:35–6)

The politics of politics

In Norway, the impact of the women's movement on public life has been considerable, greater, perhaps, than in any other western country. At the time of writing (1992), the three major political parties have women at the top: Gro Harlem Brundtland is prime minister and leader of the Labour party, Kaci Kullmann Five heads the Conservative party and Anne Enger Lahnstein the Centre (formerly agrarian) party. Dr Brundtland now heads her third government, and has caught the world's attention with a number of feminist 'firsts', such as the first cabinet featuring a majority of women ministers. Women have also moved in numbers into other previously male-dominated professions: the medical field, the priesthood, education. The private economy, however, is proving resistant to female invasion, and the domain of international trade has remained an almost exclusively male enclave. 'An age-old division of labour is resurfacing in Norway', writes the *Economist*. 'The men are out foraging while the women keep house' (23 March 1991:58).

According to the same article ('Women left, right and centre'), the feminisation of the public professions in Norway has been accompanied by a downgrading of the public in relation to the private sector: the social status of the former has diminished, and so, in relative terms, have the salaries. The trend to undermine the status of what have now become the female professions was confirmed by a report published in Oslo in 1987. 'Women', it warns, 'may be moving from a marginal minority to a marginal majority' (ibid.:58).

What is the relevance of this story to the subject of reflexive fiction? One could perhaps produce a reflexive reading of the Norwegian tale, stressing, for example, the role of mediation (a government report quoted by a financial journal quoted by a Norwegian critic and feminist) and question the political motivations behind each telling. The main point I wish to make, however, is that the whole notion of 'politics' is on shifting ground in this story: on the one hand it means gender politics, on the other party politics (left, right and centre) and the nature of government. Last but not least it means the manipulation of power which can turn a seeming victory into a defeat. A number of critics have pointed out that contemporary politics has diversified in ways that make traditional oppositions such as left/right and revolutionary/reactionary difficult to sustain (see, for example, Ross, 1988:xiv–xvi). These oppositions, a legacy of the strong influence of Marxism on political criticism, cannot without difficulty accommodate the oppositional politics of, for example, feminism. Factors such as gender, race, class and sexual orientation cut across other political categories and do not allow for a politics of simple contrasts: one cannot assume, for example, that feminists and the working class will have the same political interests or agenda. A *redefinition* of politics is under way, a deconstruction of older political categories and a displacement of the agencies of political power. The complexity of contemporary politics demands strategies of interpretation capable of seeing beyond surface meaning to discover other messages, other political implications. The politics of politics frequently consists in parading one meaning in order to disguise another. Politics in this sense becomes a textual construct which, like the literary text, responds differently to different politics of reading.

If 'real' politics is subject to paradox, recuperation and lateral manoeuvring, how much more should we suspect the politics of the literary text to be complex and deceptive. The relationship between literature and politics has been at the centre of critical debate in recent years, particularly in the context of postmodernism and its multiple affiliations with historical and political realities. The debate has produced a number of views and positions which are pertinent to literary texts and useful for their analysis; it has also, as I see it, exposed two major fallacies. The first fallacy consists in simply equating literature, or any other art form, with 'political action'. As Alain Robbe-Grillet wrote in 1957:

> that generous but utopian way of talking about a novel, a painting, or a statue as if they might count for as much in everyday action as a strike, a mutiny, or the cry of a victim denouncing his executioners, is a disservice, ultimately, to both Art and Revolution. (Robbe-Grillet, 1965:38)

There are circumstances, of course, in which a literary text counts for a great deal *more* than a strike or a cry in terms of political significance, but the contexts of literature are complex and variable and so, consequently, is its politics. The second fallacy consists in taking the opposite stance: a denial that any connection can be forged between the world and the text. Literature according to this view is by its very nature apolitical and ahistorical; the absence of direct reference disqualifies literary language from any interaction with external realities. Such a position, which, as we have seen, frequently crops up in the discussion of reflexive fiction, stems from an extremely narrow conception of terms such as 'reality' and 'politics'. It is as if only 'brute' facts and objects can be real, and only physical action political. The linguistic and fictional aspects of our realities are ignored, or at least put in a category entirely separate from the 'purely' fictional. In a society dominated by electronic media whose politics, it would seem, consists in deliberately confusing the real and the fictional, this position must strike us as very odd indeed.

Reflexivity and postmodernism

The debate surrounding fictional reflexivity in its relationship to politics has been both enriched and problematised by its assimilation, over the last twenty years or so, to the postmodernism debate. The relationship between metafiction and postmodernism is itself a problematic issue. Postmodernism is perhaps best characterised as an epistemological crisis which has touched the western world in the period since World War II. It is generally perceived as a project of *denaturalisation*: a recognition of the provisional, conventional and fabricated nature of all cultural and social structures. Postmodernism is not limited to the artistic domain: its best-known theorists (Jean-François Lyotard, Jürgen Habermas and Jean Baudrillard) present postmodernism as a phenomenon touching all aspects of contemporary life. There can be little doubt, however, that art (its creation, criticism and theorising) has proved the most fertile ground for developing and debating the ideas and issues raised by what Lyotard (1984) calls 'the postmodern condition'.

The reflexive moment (a recognition of the 'fictionality' of all social and cultural systems) is central to most definitions of postmodernism, and metafiction, defined as fiction recognising its own fictionality, has been construed as the 'natural' translation of postmodernism into literary form. Indeed, the terms 'postmodernist fiction' and 'metafiction' have frequently been used synonymously. Linda Hutcheon, for example, explains in her preface to the paperback edition of *Narcissistic Narrative* (1984) that she initially resisted the label 'postmodernist fiction' and preferred that of 'metafiction'. She concedes, however, that the former has now become dominant, and her later books on the subject are entitled *A Poetics of Postmodernism* and *The Politics of Postmodernism*. Her definition of postmodern fiction is 'historiographic metafiction'.

The popularity of the terms 'postmodernism' and 'postmodern fiction' has undoubtedly contributed to a certain decline in the use of other terms, like 'metafiction', to designate contemporary reflexive fiction. Most of the texts discussed in *this* book are generally classified as 'postmodern', and postmodernism is sometimes made to include categories of critical and theoretical writing such as post-structuralism as well. The problem with the postmodernist label is precisely that it has become *too* inclusive and indeterminate: it has been made to stand for so many aspects of contemporary life that it can no longer be used to designate a specific phenomenon such as reflexive fiction. Reflexivity, however central, is only one of a number of characteristics associated with postmodern fiction, and, perhaps even more problematically, it is not a feature exclusive to fiction of the postmodern era: many critics agree that modernist art was characterised by an intense artistic self-consciousness which cannot be clearly differentiated from postmodern reflexivity, and some, as we have seen, argue that reflexivity is and has been a feature of literary texts of all periods and all genres.

The concept of postmodernism has been so intensely debated that its meaning has become irrevocably plural. John Frow in his recent book *What Was Postmodernism?* suggests that 'the word can be taken as designating nothing more and nothing less than a genre of theoretical writing' (1991:3). The debate about postmodernism has *become* postmodernism—in itself a telling example of reflexive logic. It has also, Frow notes, become characteristic of this debate to deny any reality-value to the concept itself: 'the only thing that is anomalous about this is that the denial goes on being made in an ever-swelling flood of essays and books' (ibid.:4–5). But if, on the one hand, the *term* postmodernism has become problematised to the point where it can no longer be used to designate a particular genre, or mode, of fictional writing, it is postmodernism as *mode of investigation* which has provided the theoretical framework, the 'tools' enabling us to analyse the function of reflexivity and its effect on our reading and writing practices. The circular logic of the reflexive text affects the postmodern enterprise in its entirety, but, by turning on itself, postmodernism throws light on the many cultural artefacts which, like metafiction, have become associated with it.

The politics of reflexivity: left, right or centre?

'Once you have granted the existence, or the problematic existence, or the pseudo-existence of the concept of postmodernism', writes

John Frow, 'the genre allows you to associate it with any political position whatsoever' (ibid.:7). Frow's observations are equally valid for the concept of reflexivity; indeed, the perceived political contents of postmodernism are often a function of the critic's interpretation of reflexivity.

Early commentators on metafiction like Robert Alter and Robert Scholes stressed the introspective, self-centred strain of the genre, which in their view prevents the reflexive text's involvement with things other than its own processes. Narcissistic, elitist, and fundamentally apolitical, metafiction, in their account, robs its material of any extra-textual reference: 'This is not to say that the self-conscious novel is unable to tolerate any political materials, only that they must be made into grist for a novelistic mill with no ultimate extra-literary aims' (Alter, 1975:85). Through the anthropomorphic meta-language (self-conscious, introspective, narcissistic) of this type of criticism, fictional reflexivity is assimilated with psychological self-centredness and often represented as a shameful, almost pathological condition, a shying away from responsibility. Reflexivity, according to such a reading, is a sign of fiction's abandonment of the humanist values associated with realism, its loss of vital links with history, reality, and truth. Postmodernist fiction has been characterised in similar terms: it is, in the words of Charles Newman, 'radical aesthetically, largely apolitical and ahistorical, and in its relation of even the most terrifying matters, purportedly value-free' (1985:172–3).

According to the Marxist critic Fredric Jameson, postmodernism's seemingly apolitical disregard for history in fact masks its complicity with late capitalism. Reflexivity in his formulation becomes the function of a backward-looking imprisonment in old styles, an inability to break free, to reach out to a referent beyond the work of art itself:

> Hence, once again, pastiche: in a world in which stylistic innovation is no longer possible, all that is left is to imitate dead styles, to speak through the masks and with the voices of the styles in the imaginary museum. But this means that contemporary or postmodernist art is going to be about art itself in a new kind of way; even more, it means that one of its essential

messages will involve the necessary failure of art and the aesthetic, the failure of the new, the imprisonment in the past . . . Cultural production has been driven back inside the mind, within the monadic subject: it can no longer look directly out of its eyes at the real world for the referent but must, as in Plato's cave, trace its mental images of the world on its confining walls. (Jameson, 1983:115–16,118)

Intertextual practices in the postmodern text can only, in Jameson's view, function as pastiche, a neutral imitation which lacks the politically subversive potential of parody. The loss of a stable sense of reality means that art and life are caught in the logic of the simulacrum which in late capitalism takes the form of commodity fetishism. Terry Eagleton writes:

To say that social reality is pervasively commodified is to say that it is always already 'aesthetic'—textured, packaged, fetishized, libidinalized; and for art to reflect reality is then for it to do no more than mirror itself, in a cryptic self-referentiality which is indeed one of the inmost structures of the commodity fetish. The commodity is less an image in the sense of a 'reflection' than an image of itself, its entire material being devoted to its own self-presentation; and in such a condition the most authentically representational art becomes, paradoxically, the anti-representational artefact whose contingency and facticity figures the fate of all late-capitalist objects. If the unreality of the artistic image mirrors the unreality of its society as a whole, then this is to say that it mirrors nothing real and so does not really mirror at all. (Eagleton, 1985:62)

If many influential critics from both the political right (Gerald Graff, Charles Newman) and the political left (Fredric Jameson, Terry Eagleton) unite in condemning the reflexive postmodern text for its inability or unwillingness to engage with political realities, an increasing number of commentators seek to forge different links between radical literary practices and radical politics. Inspired by the post-structuralist theories of Roland Barthes and Michel Foucault, as well as by earlier theorists and writers such as Mikhail Bakhtin and Bertholt Brecht, they argue that reflexivity does *not* prevent political involvement. On the contrary, by calling attention to its own processes of mediation and construction, the reflexive text points to the cultural and ideological codes which inform the construct we call 'reality'. It therefore works, as Linda Hutcheon argues, to '"dedoxify" our cultural representations and their undeniable political import' (1989:3). Denaturalising cultural conventions, reflexivity then becomes the tool of a radical cultural critique, a critique aimed at unmasking our modes of representation and their ideologically constructed centres: 'Truth', 'Man', 'History', 'Reality', 'Literature'. The mode of realism, on the other hand, glossing over its own codes in an effort to give the illusion of reality, becomes, in the formulation of Catherine Belsey, 'the accomplice of ideology' (1980:73). Reading a realist text is ultimately reassuring, not because it reflects the world, but because it echoes the cultural conventions that are familiar to us, those of liberal humanism (closure, objectivity, individualism, coherence). Conversely, the reflexive text, by highlighting the 'constructedness' of texts *and* their contexts, liberates the reader to intervene, politically, in these processes. In *The Politics of Reflexivity*, Robert Siegle aligns realism with aristocratic and capitalist social structures and declares reflexivity to be 'a proletarian theory'. 'Reflexivity', he writes, 'is a permanently revolutionary dimension of literature that persists in resisting the yoke of any paradigm that attempts to obscure its own self-transforming qualities' (Siegle, 1986:244,247).

The radical (in Siegle's formulation, Marxist) political content of the reflexive mode has in its turn been challenged by critics wary of ascribing political meaning to literary form. Chris Baldick, for example, writes in a review of Patricia Waugh's book on metafiction in the 'New Accents' series:

> Among today's theoreticians of post-modern writing, some remarkable legends about the Dark Ages of nineteenth-century realist fiction have been allowed to gain currency. It can now go almost without saying that the objective of realist fiction was to inhibit any questioning of the world, to induce complacency and stupefying ideological amnesia. To Roland Barthes it meant 'a totalitarian ideology of the referent', no less. Patricia Waugh, who quotes this phrase in *Metafiction*, goes on to claim that in realist

writing 'textual contradictions are always finally resolved' at the level of plot. Once realism has been reduced to 'closure', then any other fictional mode can be made to stand for openness, life, liberty and the pursuit of happiness itself. Such themes, exasperating to any appreciative reader of nineteenth-century fiction, have surfaced frequently in Methuen's otherwise stimulating New Accents series, and the very subject of this book is an open invitation to rehearse them. (Baldick, 1985:295)

A great number of writers, including Patricia Waugh in the book reviewed by Baldick, in fact recognise the difficulty of generalising about the politics of literary forms: 'An issue which is of crucial importance, and which may only be resolved once post-modernism has itself become a 'post'' phenomenon, is the question of the *politically* 'radical' status of *aesthetically* radical texts' (Waugh, 1984:148).

Another way of accounting for the politics of the reflexive postmodern text is to recognise the coexistence of both radical and conservative impulses. Linda Hutcheon (1988, 1989) refers to the politics of postmodernist fiction, or 'historiographic metafiction', as she calls it, as double-coded: 'complicitous critique' or 'authorised transgression'. What she means by this is not always clear. Sometimes she refers to the 'dedoxifying' effect of the reflexive enquiry and its intrinsic capacity for radical political questioning; elsewhere, she sets up a paradoxical relation between the *reflexive* dimension, regarded as politically neutral, and the text's *historical* engagement, which tends to be radical. She also establishes a clear distinction between postmodern texts, the politics of which is always compromised, and more overtly political literature, such as feminist writing. The status of texts which are *both* feminist and postmodern thus becomes uncertain: if such texts exist at all, their politics must be very complex indeed.

The problematic politics of the postmodern text has prompted some critics to posit two kinds of postmodernism, and two kinds of reflexive politics. Hal Foster in his introduction to *The Anti-Aesthetic* distinguishes between a postmodernism of reaction and a postmodernism of resistance, and E. Ann Kaplan in *Postmodernism and Its Discontents* differentiates a 'utopian' postmodernism from a commercial or 'co-opted' one. The adoption of postmodern techniques such as reflexivity for commercial purposes in advertisements and popular culture certainly makes it difficult to argue for an intrinsically subversive postmodern quality. In *Realism and Power* Alison Lee tries to overcome this difficulty by claiming that 'serious' postmodern fiction uses metafictional techniques to subvert structures of authority, whereas popular culture makes use of the same techniques to 'mask an essentially Realist ideology' (1990:139). The techniques are the same, she claims, but the motivation behind their use, and so their political import, is different. Her argument is undoubtedly correct in its conclusion that the political content of, say, a novel by Salman Rushdie is in sharp contrast to that of a cigarette advertisement, but it is problematic in its insistence that the ideological content of reflexivity nevertheless remains essentially subversive, and that of realism conservative.

Much of the critical disagreement concerning the politics of postmodernism and the politics of reflexivity hinges on questions of definition. If reflexivity is understood as purely literary introspection it is not surprising to see its politics defined as neutral or complicit. If politics is regarded as the realm of action rather than ideas, the literary text, especially the often difficult postmodern text, is unlikely to qualify as an adequate political tool. If the label postmodernism is reserved for a category of radically anti-realist works, it must appear irrelevant to historical and political realities. If, on the contrary, a critic wishes to salvage postmodernism for political radicalism, he or she will include in this category the kinds of writing that combine reflexive techniques with an awareness of extra-textual realities. Many critics have taken the American 'surfiction' of the sixties and seventies and the French 'new novel' to epitomise postmodernist writing, but Linda Hutcheon (1988:40) classifies them as instances of late modernist extremism, arguing that their self-reflection is inward-oriented only; *truly* postmodern texts also have the function of demasking cultural codes or ideological paradigms. By making this classification, Hutcheon seems prepared to accept that the radical critique of subjectivity, perception and representation at work in such texts is not political, or not political according to her preferred sense of the term.

When debating questions of textual politics, most critics focus on the text itself, seeking to determine the political meaning of a particular mode, or category, of writing. But, as every politician knows, politics is an interactive enterprise; its ultimate meaning lies not so much in the message as in its effect, the reaction of its audience. The reason postmodern or reflexive texts have been interpreted in such widely different ways should perhaps be sought in the interaction between *textual* strategies and strategies of *reading*. Reflexive strategies are complex, generally calling for a double, or ironic, mode of reading. Discourses are framed, or quoted, and the role of mediation foregrounded. The 'message' is bracketed, and the reader put in a position of having to decide how it is to be read. An ironic reading, subversive of the quoted discourse, is generally possible, but, as in all ironic reading contracts, subversion depends on an initial recognition of the bracketed meaning. Moreover, and this is Jameson's point, irony and parody, in order to be subversive, require a stable position from which the quoted discourse can be regarded as an aberration. Postmodern writing, according to Jameson, fails to provide a linguistic or political norm against which quoted discourse can be judged, and the quotation must therefore be neutral, pastiche, deprived of parody's subversive potential. The reader's role in determining textual politics is not accorded a central place in Jameson's construction. But the power of textual interpretation must, finally, reside with the reader. Parody, as David Bennett points out, 'is the effect of a particular, intertextual strategy of reading' (1985:28). The interpretation of the complex ironies of the postmodern text depends on the various contexts surrounding the act of interpretation, not least of which is the political persuasion of the reader her- or himself.

Alain Robbe-Grillet's story 'The Secret Room', discussed in Chapter 3, illustrates the ambiguous interpretative and political positioning offered the reader of the reflexive text. The narrative is literally framed: it is presented as the description of a painting. The real frame, however, is the voice of the narrator, the man viewing (or fantasising) the scene depicted on the canvas. The story is also framed by implicit intertextual reference to the genre of gothic horror. As a male sexual fantasy which calls attention to its own constructedness, 'The Secret Room' can be read as a critique of the stories, and the fantasies, to which it alludes. But it is also possible to regard it as complicit with the genre it quotes: the reader is drawn into the frame, invited to occupy the position of the narrator in relation to elements in the story. Moreover, it is a story which offers no alternative to the sexual fantasy it invokes: there is no 'real' painting which can be seen as a corrective to the distorted view of the narrator—indeed, as we have seen, there is no reality against which to measure the fabricated illusion of the artistic image, narrative or visual. 'The Secret Room' leaves open a number of interpretative choices: if one decides to analyse it from a feminist position (which seems its most relevant political context), it can be read, depending on the strategy of the reader, as either subversive of, or complicit with, the male perspective it presents. It is also possible to regard the story as politically irrelevant or neutral: not only in that it offers no alternative, but also in that it deliberately distances itself from any putative 'real'. Linda Hutcheon's distinction between postmodern fiction and overtly political literature undoubtedly holds good for this reading of Robbe-Grillet's story: its politics is multiply coded, brought out only in specific responses to its textual strategies. The question remains whether it is impossible, as she claims, for a postmodern text to have a clear (oppositional) politics, not compromised by its complicity with the disputed modes of representation.

While many feminists have regarded postmodernism as irrelevant to their cause, one branch of feminist criticism has welcomed the postmodern denaturalisation of cultural systems and put it to use in its own critique of patriarchal structures. If gender, sexuality and the human 'self' are regarded as constructed rather than natural, the possibility is open for a radical reconstruction of these concepts according to different ideologies: the 'fictions' of human life can be regendered. This process of gender deconstruction and redefinition is traced in a number of reflexive feminist novels. Jeanette Winterson's *Sexing the Cherry* combines history (seventeenth-century *and* contemporary London), fantasy and fairy tale to question received notions of gender and love as well as truth and reality. Gender is represented as a burden from which both men and women long to escape. The Dog-Woman, by virtue of her size and strength excluded from a conventional female sexual identity, occupies a pivotal position outside the boundaries of 'normal' human existence. Her adopted son Jordan is not so lucky. Burdened by his assigned gender, tortured by romantic love, he sets out on a voyage through a multitude of realities, destined, it would seem, to destabilise any sense of what is true, real or natural. He comes across a city where romantic love is considered a plague and made illegal. Unfortunately, there is no cure for the illness. The 'happily ever after' of conventional fairy tales is deconstructed—twelve times—as the twelve dancing princesses in turn tell him how their marriages to the twelve princes failed. Jordan goes on pursuing his lost love, the elusive youngest princess but, when she refuses him, realises that she is a projection of his own desire, a lost 'self' which can only exist in his dreams. The vision of a different mode of engendering, outside the norms of 'natural' procreation and socialisation, is illustrated by the image of grafting and related to the emblematic use of fruit to designate the narrators. Just as the narrators themselves (the female giant and the son she fishes out of the stinking Thames) are distanced from naturalised models of reproduction and sexual behaviour, so the exotic fruit they are associated with (bananas, pineapples) are perceived as 'unnatural' when first introduced to England. The practice of grafting, or procreation without seed or parent, is also condemned as unnatural, but succeeds in creating new and improved species of fruit. Despite his mother's warning that things not born from seed 'had no gender and were a confusion to themselves' (Winterson, 1989:79), Jordan is able to show her that the grafted cherry, 'born' of unnatural sexual practices, is no monster but a healthy female tree. He regrets that the method is not applicable to human beings. Jordan's regret, however, is Winterson's opportunity. In the overall context of *Sexing the Cherry*, all manner of productive transgression is possible. The process of grafting is at work at several levels in the story, in the redefinition of gender, self and sexual practices, in the fusion of history and fantasy, in the grafting of Jordan and the Dog-Woman on to twentieth-century characters. Repeatedly, the novel takes existing material and creates it anew, according to different ideologies and different modes of writing. The political implications seem unambiguous: a critique of naturalised social and sexual practices, a vision of differently 'sexed' roles for both males and females. The lack of a stable grounding in reality or nature for any ideology of sex or truth does not disempower the characters or blunt the 'message'—on the contrary. In the embedded tale of the floating town, gravity is suspended, but the inhabitants learn to live happily without it, preferring their airborne freedom to the confinements of life on the ground. As an allegory for the suspension of grounding certainties such as 'truth' and 'reality', the tale projects an optimistic view of ungrounded existence: it can be experienced as liberation rather than loss.

The politics of *Sexing the Cherry* is consistent with that of post-structuralist feminism: it locates the oppression of both women and men in naturalised ideologies of gender and explores alternative modes of defining sexual identity. To argue that the politics of this postmodern novel is, by necessity, compromised, seems beside the point: in the context of a particular political discourse, the text clearly signals its position, and its postmodern (reflexive) textual strategies work to underpin the postmodern vision it embodies. It it equally true, however, that this text, like all literary texts, can be recontextualised, placed in a context which fundamentally alters its political implications. It is always possible for readers to reappropriate textual strategies for their own political or interpretative purposes; moreover, textual politics is also a function of the text's mode of circulation, its status as commodity. The literary text exists in a complex intertextual, cultural and economic network of publishers, critics, teaching institutions and visual media, all contributing to its significance. The politics of the text can never be isolated from the multiple and variable contexts surrounding the act of reading.

The politics of metafiction

> Who writes? For whom is the writing being done? In what circumstances? These, it seems to me, are the questions whose answers provide us with the ingredients making for a politics of interpretation. (Said, 1983:135)

To Edward Said's questions one could add others: Who reads? In what circumstances is the reading being done? Who comments on the text? How is the text construed critically in terms of its mode and genre? What critical discourses shape its interpretation? What institutional practices frame the critical enterprise? The last part of this chapter will examine the impact of some of these questions on the politics of metafiction.

The politics of the reflexive text in the first instance depends on the text's reflexivity being recognised as such, and this, as we have seen, is frequently the function of certain strategies of reading. If the reflexive dimension hinges on an ironic contract with the reader (who is asked to read against the grain of the quoted discourse), it is always possible for the contract to fail, and the text's meaning, and politics, to be received unreflexively. It would perhaps be easy to dismiss such a reception as simple misreading, signalling a lack of discernment on the part of the reader, but the fact is that postmodern texts frequently fail to signpost their ironic or parodic intentions clearly, and so tend to confound even experienced readers. The context of reception in such cases becomes the determining factor: the more ambiguous the textual contract, the more dependent on contextual circumstances its reading becomes.

To illustrate this kind of textual ambiguity, I have chosen an image from the novel *Holden's Performance* by Murray Bail: the vomit map of Australia. The map comes into existence as Holden, the main character, is evicting a drunken geography teacher from a Manly picture-theatre. Before Holden can reach the street with his disorderly charge, the man goes limp in his hands and deposits the contents of his much abused stomach on the carpet in the foyer. The vile produce, to Holden's amazement, takes on a life of its own and spreads until it reaches an unmistakable shape—Australia—complete to the most minute detail, from the apple isle to the blowflies buzzing around the Northern Territory. Alex Screech, the entrepreneurial owner of the picture-theatre, is quick to recognise the commercial value of the map, which is promptly framed and exhibited, to the delight of the picture-goers, who see in it a token of their own patriotism.

In my (reflexive) reading of the vomit map, the image stands as a comment on the frequently absurd cultural practices associated with the creation of national identities: the use of icons, often in the form of maps, to mobilise a sense of nationhood; the construction of stereotypes (Australian high-spirited drunkenness and ingenuity) to account for national characteristics. This kind of cultural map-making is exposed throughout *Holden's Performance*, most notably in the figure of Holden himself, characterised as the very embodiment of 'the qualities which have put this country on the map' (Bail, 1987:353). Holden is, of course, a textual rather than 'natural' product of his country: as a young man he was daily and literally fed on a diet consisting of galley proofs from the Adelaide *Advertiser* (mixed with his breakfast cereal, spread on sandwiches and blended into his mashed potatoes). Deconstructed through reflexive double-coding, images such as these subvert the practices they mimic, inviting readers to examine the cultural (and commercial) production of national symbols and its ideological implications.

The parodic element of *Holden's Performance* can also be seen to support another, non-reflexive reading. The temptation is there, throughout, to read the text as a more direct parody, not of the processes of cultural construction, but of the Australian 'character' itself, in which case the stereotypes are not so much deconstructed as reinforced. The political implications of such a reading are, obviously, very different. *Holden's Performance* is a good example of the kind of postmodern text which, as Hutcheon argues, embodies a paradoxical political position, at once complicit and subversive. Its subversive potential in this case depends for its realisation on whether the text is recognised as reflexive. The interpretation of the novel by individual readers is less likely, I think, to reflect textual ambiguity. Contextual factors such as intertextual experience, familiarity with the stereotypes invoked and attitude towards them will, inevitably, predispose the reader towards one or the other of the politically opposed interpretative choices.

By classifying Bail's novel as reflexive or non-reflexive, we change not only the text's mode, but its politics. Isolating the reflexive factor from other textual elements, and metafiction, as a distinct genre, from other categories of writing, are critical choices which may in themselves have a political import. Our very *definition* of reflexivity may betoken our textual politics. Definitions, oppositions and generic distinctions are perhaps not functions of the texts they seek to classify so much as products of a critical will to power, the desire to impose a certain politics on literary texts. Realism and reflexivity, for example, may be constituted as incompatible, not because this opposition is carried out by textual analysis but in order to validate the critic's own preferences and justify her/his critical methods. As we have noted, many critics isolate reflexivity in order to dismiss it summarily and glorify texts they regard as non-reflexive. Significantly, many of the synonyms for reflexive fiction carry a negative connotation: introspective fiction, narcissistic fiction, self-conscious fiction, anti-fiction, problematic fiction, masturbatory fiction. There is a tendency, with authors who disapprove of reflexivity, to reject it without bothering to examine it, find out what it is actually about. The fictional 'self', as reflected in metafiction, can be scorned as an object unworthy of critical enquiry; little attention is given the fact that this object is hardly a 'self' at all, but a number of processes of mediation and representation, none of which exists in isolation from other textual and contextual factors. Conversely, critics who regard reflexivity as an agent of liberation, freeing fictional narrative from the 'tyranny' of realist representation, have a tendency to overlook the reflexive dimension of much realist fiction. In order for binary oppositions such as reflexive/realist to be upheld, texts must be made to fit into our ready-made categories, even if this means sacrificing critical accuracy for the sake of critical politics.

When a type of writing is created or discovered, the way metafiction was discovered in the sixties and seventies and postmodern writing at about the same time, something happens which affects the body of literature in its entirety. The processes of definition and inclusion create another category of texts, the excluded, defined as lacking the qualities characterising the new genre. A process of unification occurs, for texts which previously were seen to have nothing in common are now unified by their non-reflexivity, or their non-postmodernity. A new binarism has come into being, which, it would seem, inevitably implies a certain hierarchy of values: reflexivity—good, realism—bad, or vice versa, or modernism—good, postmodernism—bad, and so on. The negative, or 'straw term', as Jameson (1975—76:234) calls it, can then be used to designate everything that is in political, logical or ethical error. Metafiction, a genre frequently associated with intellectual sophistication, modernity, radical rupture with tradition, difficulty and instability, demanded by contrast a literature asserting the values of tradition, a simpler, more stable and natural kind of writing against which its literary pyrotechnics could be displayed. The elitist strain of metafiction or postmodern fiction called for its 'other' to be more democratic, more accessible, but perhaps, at least to critics embracing the new genre, just a bit dull. The straw term for postmodernism has, depending on the critic, been construed as either modernism or realism; in the case of metafiction, it is generally realism. A number of feminist critics have moreover noted a tendency to associate postmodernism's straw term with our culture's favoured 'other', the feminine (see, for example, Polan, 1988). Not only is non-postmodern writing regarded as possessing the stable, rather unadventurous qualities women are conventionally supposed to represent, but postmodern writers, it would seem, are almost invariably male. Indeed, if we are to believe most books on postmodern fiction (or metafiction), the genre has until very recently remained the preserve of male writers, and, with the exception of a few daredevils in South America, it has been confined to European and North American centres of culture. One is tempted to construct a political fable based on our tale of Norwegian politics: as the women's movement gained ground, and women writers and feminist critics threatened to destabilise the literary canon, moving in numbers to occupy the limited amount of seats available in the parliaments and cabinets of university courses, publisher's lists and bookshop displays, it may have seemed politically expedient, for men, to make an oblique move, risking the competitive international climate of the latest literary fad, and promoting it as intellectually superior and more sophisticated than the pleasant, but after all rather housewifely activity taken over by the women. Judging by the amount of critical attention accorded this kind of writing, one must concede that the move has been politically astute.

While theoretically seductive, my fable cannot claim the unassailable status of truth. On the one hand, the absence of women and minority writers from the postmodern canon may indicate the privileging of male and white writers in most critical accounts, on the other, it is also possible that women writers for a long time *actually* shunned postmodernism, leaving this newly discovered high-tech plaything to the boys. The more recent inclusion of such writers as Angela Carter, Margaret Atwood, Toni Morrison and Salman Rushdie makes it clear that many women and non-white writers today *do* write reflexively (and that there are critics prepared to consider them), but it could be, as Patricia Waugh suggests in *Feminine Fictions*, that many marginalised writers have had a different agenda, both literary and political, and so have chosen to express themselves in different modes. Whatever the true explanatory force of this particular fable, it should make it clear that our critical constructions are not politically innocent; our very genres and oppositions may have a hidden agenda. If it is true, as Andrew Ross puts it, that postmodern politics

> has been posed as a politics of difference, wherein many of the voices of color, gender, and sexual orientation, newly liberated from the margins, have found representation under conditions that are not exclusively tailored to the hitherto heroicized needs and interests of white, male intellectuals and/or white, male workers (Ross, 1988:xvi)

it is also true that the postmodernist text through its critical and cultural contexts can be made to carry a very different political message.

In order to assess the politics of literature accurately, criticism needs to examine, reflexively, its own practices and identify their politics. The metalanguage of metafiction testifies to the pertinence of this type of analysis. The constitution of the genre and the binary contrasts it enables offer potential for political manoeuvring. The terminology associated with reflexivity is not, as we have seen, neutral; it misleadingly identifies such writing as derivative, egotistical and often morally reprehensible. The anthropomorphic nature of the 'self' in terms such as 'self-conscious', 'introspective' and 'narcissistic' constitutes an identity for fiction which is not only human but regarded as coherent and unified; a moral and psychological entity very much in tune with Christian and humanist notions of 'self', but curiously discrepant when considered in conjunction with the often fragmented, unstable, multi-layered texts it supposedly designates. Moreover, like 'Man', the text is identified as gendered space, often functioning through its own imagery as well as in the metalanguage of its commentary as a series of relationships between gendered agents.

The assimilation of sexual and textual intercourse has become a commonplace in much critical commentary. In *Fabulation and Metafiction* Robert Scholes offers this definition for what he calls 'the orgastic pattern of fiction':

> The archetype of all fiction is the sexual act. In saying this I do not mean merely to remind the reader of the connection between all art and the erotic in human nature . . . For what connects fiction—and music—with sex is the fundamental orgastic rhythm of tumescence and detumescence, of tension and resolution, of intensification to the point of climax and consummation. In the sophisticated forms of fiction, as in the sophisticated practice of sex, much of the art consists of delaying climax within the framework of desire in order to prolong the pleasurable act itself (Scholes, 1979:26).

The sexual metaphor for fictional creation and reception has figured prominently in metafiction (most notably in writers such as John Barth and William Gass); it has also been much exploited by literary critics and theorists. But the pleasure of the text as represented in this and other formulations is gender-specific: the orgastic pattern of fiction is based on male sexuality. Texts and analyses based on female pleasure, Susan Winnett observes, 'might have a different plot' (1990:507).

According to the most common versions of the sexual model for the narrative act, the author is male, the active and creative partner inseminating the blank page or acting on the receptive mind or passive body of the reader, generally represented as female. John Fowles's *Mantissa* parodies this pattern in a number of ways. The male character Miles is the author; the female character performs a number of different roles. She is muse, inspiring the author through sexual ministrations, then providing a receptive womb for his creative output. Their intercourse is presented as simultaneous coitus and birth, the offspring of their efforts the 'lovely little story' in which they both figure. In other versions of the intercourse Erato is the reader of Miles's fiction, variously seduced or offended by what she reads. Or she is a character, the female character the male author invariably loves and always tries to create anew. She is also (and this is where *Mantissa*'s self-parodic distance is evident) a feminist critic who ridicules the self-indulgent sexual fantasy of the author, but is ridiculed in her turn for her short-sighted sexual politics. *Mantissa* is a novel whose textual politics is infinitely and deliberately problematised; but whatever its actual political message, it is a text which, through the literalisation of the sexual metaphor for fictional creation, exposes the gendered politics of its own metalanguage.

Commenting on the sexist division of labour in Calvino's *If On a Winter's Night a Traveller*, Teresa de Lauretis writes:

> The vision of woman as passive capacity, receptivity, readiness to receive—a womb waiting to be fecundated by words (*his* words), a void ready to be filled with meanings, or elsewhere a blank page awaiting insemination by the writer's pen—is a notorious cliché of Western literary writing. (de Lauretis, 1987:75)

Feminist critics have also commented on the metaphorical usage of sexuality, woman and the feminine as rhetorical space in the writing of dominant French post-structuralist theorists such as Roland Barthes, Julia Kristeva and Jacques Derrida. While it is possible, as post-structuralist feminism has shown, to press the theoretical valorisation of 'otherness' or 'difference' into the service of feminist politics, there is no necessary link between the feminine 'other' of such theorising and the actual lives of women: the kinds of writing coded as 'feminine' are in fact generally written by men. In *Gynesis* Alice Jardine speculates about what will happen when 'women take over this discourse in the name of woman' (1985:263). This is precisely the project in which many women writers and critics are currently engaged. The writing of Jeanette Winterson offers numerous examples of a literary space otherwise gendered: visions of homo-erotic love, procreation through the process of grafting, gendered identity freed from the tyranny of the male/female binarism. The language of 'pornosophy' is here appropriated for a politics of gender which subverts the heterosexual, androcentred norm.

A reflexive commentary on literary politics must inevitably return to its own political agenda(s), and the time has come to question the emphasis on gender politics in my own discussion and acknowledge its necessary blindspots. Given the particular contexts surrounding reflexive fiction and academic criticism, the feminist intervention which can exist on this ground is generally confined to white middle-class women; and their oppositional discourses are always in danger of being perceived, by other groups, as signifying just another form of white dictation or elitist orthodoxy. The concept of 'politics' is itself likely to be perceived differently depending on the political circumstances of the perceiver, and in the discrepancy between different notions of what constitutes textual politics lies a constant potential for conflict. Ross Chambers discusses the problem which arises when oppositional literary discourse adopts the mode of 'bearing witness', offering direct access to truth. The ideology he associates with this mode is that of 'dictation'; it is dictatorial in the sense that it wants to control its own meaning (Chambers, 1990:201). Unlike the reflexive text which calls attention to the constructed nature of all truths, the dictatorial text seeks to impose on the reader its own version of what is true and just. But it is also possible to argue that to proclaim a 'truth' which challenges another and dominant 'truth' in many circumstances constitutes a more effective political move than a textual strategy based on the deconstruction of political certainties.

Surrounding the reflexive postmodern text and its criticism are institutions whose politics interferes powerfully with that of the textual construct itself. The market-driven publishing industry and the seemingly autonomous academic literary institution between them exercise a power which, it would seem, raises questions about the possibility of a truly oppositional political programme for either literature or criticism. Rather than analysing individual texts from particular political perspectives, one might, as many Marxist critics have suggested, more successfully intervene in the politics of literary communication by challenging the very notions of 'literature' and 'literary criticism'. The problem, of course, is that such challenges themselves tend to come from within the institutions they seek to subvert. An oppositional political programme for literature, it would seem, almost inevitably implies a certain amount of complicity. While it is undoubtedly true that reflexive fiction is part of, and so in one sense complicit with, the dominant literary and critical discourses defined by its institutional affiliations, it is also true that its textual strategies can become potent tools for writers and critics out to question the institutional practices by which they are themselves defined.

6

This Is Not a Conclusion

Always historicise

> 'Do you know, Mr Yule, that you have suggested a capital idea to me? If I were to take up your views, I think it isn't at all unlikely that I might make a good thing of writing against writing. It should be my literary specialty to rail against literature. The reading public should pay me for telling them that they oughtn't to read. I must think it over.'
>
> 'Carlyle has anticipated you,' threw in Alfred.
>
> 'Yes, but in an antiquated way. I would base my polemic on the newest philosophy.' (Gissing, 1968:55)

Jasper Milvain's recipe for writing contains, it would seem, the main ingredients for postmodern metafiction: writing against writing and reader abuse dressed in the garb of 'the newest philosophy'. But George Gissing's *New Grub Street*, from which this passage is taken, was published a century ago, in 1891, and it suggests that Milvain's 'capital idea' even then lacked originality: it had been anticipated by Carlyle. In his polemical book *The Post-Modern Aura* Charles Newman cites this passage in order to mock the idea that reflexivity is a specifically postmodern phenomenon. 'Those who take up the notion that Post-Modern art has suddenly become self-referential', he writes, 'commit the grossest ahistoricism, and confuse whatever claims might be made on behalf of the present' (Newman, 1985:40).

Robert Siegle, a critic much more sympathetic towards reflexive strategies than Newman, shares his view on this matter:

> I have little sympathy for discussions that seem to confine reflexivity to recent avant-garde works as if the novel had 'evolved' into metafictional cleverness sometime during the 1960s or were more an American than an English phenomenon. Reflexivity seems so 'current' mainly because poststructuralist theory allows us to understand it fully at the same time that current fictional practice has forced an at times almost reactionary critical establishment either to ignore it or to devise rather elaborate strategies for its containment. (Siegle, 1986:14)

One of the aims of the present book has been precisely to analyse some of the strategies of containment by which the critical establishment has sought to limit the extent of the reflexive enquiry and marginalise its impact on our understanding of literary texts. By arguing that fictional reflexivity is a postmodern novelty, by setting up relations of opposition and incompatibility between reflexive and realist impulses in fiction and by creating a distinct genre ('metafiction') to accommodate the phenomenon, critics have variously managed to avoid the formidable task of examining the whole of our literary tradition in light of its self-reflexive interrogation. A 'history' of fictional reflexivity, sensitive to changes in literary forms but aware of the danger of easy categorisation, is yet to be written. 'It is certain', writes Fredric Jameson,

> that we need a more adequate account of autoreferentiality in literary history than any which has previously been given: yet . . . without some more adequate historical framework, this particular phenomenon—with its suggestion of a kind of self-consciousness of the text about itself—is only too easily pressed back into the service of the old modernism/realism antinomy. (Jameson, 1975–76:232)

Perhaps the 'adequate historical framework' for an account of reflexive fiction will not come about until postmodern metafiction itself is safely relegated to a literary 'past' and can be analysed from a position of historical detachment.

The end of all metafictions

Once we knew that fiction was about life and criticism was about fiction—and everything was simple. Now we know that fiction is about other fiction, is criticism in fact, or metafiction. And we know that criticism is about the impossibility of anything being about life, really, or even about fiction, or finally, about anything. Criticism has taken away the very idea of 'aboutness' from us. It has taught us that language is tautological, if it is not nonsense, and to the extent that it is about anything, it is about itself. Mathematics is about mathematics, poetry is about poetry, and criticism is about the impossibility of its own existence. (Scholes, 1975:1)

Robert Scholes in this passage offers a parodic summary of the consequences of reflexivity for fiction as well as for other disciplines: it has problematised the idea of 'aboutness' to the extent that it is no longer possible to distinguish between a discourse and its metadiscourse. If fiction, poetry and mathematics are primarily about themselves, criticism in its turn must adopt the inward glance, investigate its own methods and its role in constituting its object of enquiry. The idea of 'aboutness' to which Scholes somewhat nostalgically refers is one which clearly distinguishes between 'inside' and 'outside' positions: fiction is 'about' life while remaining separate from it; criticism is 'about' literature but itself untainted by literary processes. The lesson of reflexivity, however, seems to be that this kind of 'aboutness' cannot exist: there can be no meta-positions, no 'outside' from which the critic, the scientist or the artist can look in on an object of study which exists in its own rights, independent of the observer. The question remains whether a different notion of 'aboutness', allowing for an awareness of the observer's role in constituting the object, can be defined. Steve Woolgar (1988:99) refers to the danger of 'ontological gerrymandering', by which he means the tendency to constitute one's own discourse according to an ideology of representation one criticises in other texts. In the case of this particular study of metafiction, a reflexive critical position has to include a recognition of the precarious balance between the deconstruction of certain conceptions of reflexive fiction and the almost inevitable tendency to construct one's own categories for its containment. Is it possible to write a book about metafiction without preserving, in some sense, the notions of 'aboutness' and 'metafiction'? Is 'reflexivity' a less restrictive label than 'metafiction', 'self-conscious fiction' or 'postmodern fiction'? Is reflexive criticism doomed to rehearse 'the impossibility of its own existence', or will it succeed in coming full circle without swallowing its own tail/tale?

If the very notion of 'aboutness' is challenged by reflexivity, the use of the label 'metafiction' to designate reflexive fiction becomes more than a little misleading: metafiction is the type of fiction which denies the possibility of any meta-positions. While metafiction abolishes the distinction between the inside and the outside of the fictional text, its *name* ironically implies that such a distinction can be made: the term metafiction preserves the critical categories the fictions themselves most emphatically undermine. Perhaps the time has come to acknowledge the metafictional paradox and to rename our fictions. Metafiction is dead, long live . . . . ! (Since it is unlikely that a critical consensus will be obtained for a new name, the reader is advised to write his/her preferred option in this space.)

. . . but it is not over yet

The birth of metafiction seems to have coincided with the death of the novel—or so it appeared to many readers of fiction and criticism in the sixties and seventies. An apocalyptic mood reigned in much literary commentary at the time: the form of the novel, it was felt, would not survive the onslaught of modernist and postmodernist experimentation. On the one hand, writers reiterated the modernist complaint that the nineteenth-century bourgeois novel was an inadequate form in which to express a twentieth-century reality; on the other, experimentation with fictional form was seen to have reached an impasse and there was simply nowhere for it to go. Metaphors of suspicion, exhaustion and death frequently accompanied discussions of the state of the novel, and reflexivity was, perhaps not surprisingly, related to the suicidal tendencies of a genre about to suffocate through its own inability to connect with its altered surroundings. But the road to silence and death, painfully charted by writers like Samuel Beckett, turned out to be longer than many critics had anticipated. The novel, however moribund, simply refused to die, and as most critics were eventually forced to admit, its narcissistic self-scrutiny was not an isolated and isolating phenomenon but a response to the intellectual climate of its time. Its seemingly sterile introspection and lack of self-confidence corresponded to the processes of reflexive denaturalisation at work in all fields of human endeavour in the postmodern era. Moreover, as post-structuralist theorising became better known and better understood, the absence of grounding certainties (in fiction, in criticism) was no longer received as life-threatening. With due regard for the provisionality of all fictions of literary history, one might advance the optimistic hypothesis that contemporary fiction, the writing of the eighties and nineties, has emerged triumphant from its clash with death. Reflexivity is no longer regarded as symptomatic of literary paralysis but has become an analytical tool in our quest to understand human realities. The modes of today's fiction are less polarised than what was the case two decades ago: reflexivity coexists happily (or paradoxically) with features of realist fiction, such as recognisably human characters and historical settings. The climate of reception has also changed as a number of reflexive texts have moved from the experimental fringe to the mainstream of literary production: today critical opinion concerning the merits of reflexive writing is still varied, but a novel is less likely to be rejected (or, for that matter, praised) simply *because* it is overtly reflexive.

The British writer B. S. Johnson illustrates the paranoia frequently associated with reflexive fiction when he bursts through the story of *Albert Angelo* (published in 1964) to explain what the novel is *really* about, namely himself:

> fuck all this lying look what im really trying to write about is writing not all this stuff about architecture trying to say something about writing about my writing im my hero though what a useless appellation my first character then im trying to say something about me through him albert an architect when whats the point in covering up. (Johnson, 1964:167)

The idea that fiction is lying here becomes an obstacle to true communication with the reader. In order to tell the truth, Johnson's narrator must leave his fiction behind, expose it as 'only a story' and try to enlist the reader's sympathy by appealing to a common reality outside the realm of fiction. By contrast, most readers and writers today share the knowledge that our realities are infused with fictions, and that stories are not lies but monuments to the search for a specifically human truth. The reflexive reminder which concludes Jeanette Winterson's *The Passion* signals a different attitude, a new confidence in the power of fiction:

I'm telling you stories. Trust me (Winterson, 1987:160).

Bibliography

Abrams, M. H. (1977) 'The Deconstructive Angel' *Critical Inquiry*, 3, Spring, 425-38

Alter, R. (1975) *Partial Magic: The Novel as a Self-Conscious Genre*, Berkeley: University of California Press

Ashmore, M. (1989) *The Reflexive Thesis: Wrighting Sociology of Scientific Knowledge*, Chicago and London: University of Chicago Press

Bail, M. (1987) *Holden's Performance*, Ringwood, Vic.: Penguin

Baldick, C. (1985) 'Estrangements' *Times Literary Supplement*, 15 March, 295

Barnes, J. (1984) *Flaubert's Parrot*, London: Picador

Barth, J. (1969) *Lost in the Funhouse*, New York: Bantam Books

—— (1979) *Letters*, New York: G. P. Putnam's Sons

Barthes, R. (1972) *Critical Essays*, trans. R. Howard, Evanston: Northwestern University Press

—— (1975a) *The Pleasure of the Text*, trans. R. Miller, New York: Hill & Wang

—— (1975b) *S/Z* , trans. R. Miller, London: Cape

—— (1977) *Image-Music-Text*, trans. S. Heath, Glasgow: Fontana

Baudrillard, J. (1988) *Selected Writings*, Cambridge: Polity Press

Bennett, D. (1985) 'Parody, Postmodernism, and the Politics of Reading' *Critical Quarterly*, 27 (4), 27-43

Belsey, C. (1980) *Critical Practice*, London and New York: Methuen

Berger, J. (1972) *Ways of Seeing*, London: British Broadcasting Corporation and Penguin Books

Borges, J. L. (1970) *Labyrinths*, Harmondsworth: Penguin

Boyd, M. (1983) *The Reflexive Novel: Fiction as Critique*, London: Associated University Presses

Brooke-Rose, C. (1981) *A Rhetoric of the Unreal: Studies in Narrative and Structure, Especially of the Fantastic*, Cambridge: Cambridge University Press

Byatt, A. S. (1990) *Possession*, London: Chatto & Windus

Calvino, I. (1992) *If On a Winter's Night a Traveller*, trans. W. Weaver, London: Minerva

Carey, P. (1981) *Exotic Pleasures*, London: Picador

—— (1986) *Illywhacker*, St Lucia: University of Queensland Press

—— (1988) *Oscar and Lucinda*, St Lucia: University of Queensland Press

Carter, A. (1984) *Nights at the Circus*, London: Chatto & Windus, The Hogarth Press

Chambers, R. (1982) 'Le texte "difficile" et son lecteur' in L. Dällenbach and J. Ricardou (eds) *Problèmes actuels de la lecture*, Paris: Éditions Clancier-Guénaud, 81-93

—— (1984) *Story and Situation: Narrative Seduction and the Power of Fiction*, Minneapolis: University of Minnesota Press

—— (1989) 'Narrative and Other Triangles' *Journal of Narrative Technique* 19 (1), Winter, 31-47

—— (1990) 'Opposition by Appropriation: Manuel Puig's *Kiss of the Spiderwoman*' *AUMLA* 74, November, 201-23

Christensen, I. (1981) *The Meaning of Metafiction*, Bergen, Oslo, Tromsø: Universitetsforlaget

Crosman, R. (1980) 'Do Readers Make Meaning?' in S. R. Suleiman and I. Crosman (eds) *The Reader in the Text*, Princeton: Princeton University Press, 149-64

Dällenbach, L. (1989) *The Mirror in the Text*, trans. J. Whiteley and E. Hughes, Cambridge: Polity Press

Daniel, H. (1988) *Liars: Australian New Novelists*, Ringwood, Vic.: Penguin

de Lauretis, T. (1987) 'Calvino and the Amazons: Reading the (Post)Modern Text' in *Technologies of Gender: Essays on*

Theory, Film and Fiction, Bloomington and Indianapolis: Indiana University Press, 76-83

de Man, P. (1983) *Blindness and Insight: Essays in the Rhetoric of Contemporary Criticism*, Minneapolis: University of Minnesota Press

Derrida, J. (1978) *Writing and Difference*, trans. A. Bass, London and Henley: Routledge & Kegan Paul

—— (1981a) *Dissemination*, trans. B. Johnson, Chicago: Chicago University Press

—— (1981b) *Positions*, trans. A. Bass, London: Athlone Press

Eagleton, T. (1985) 'Capitalism, Modernism and Postmodernism' *New Left Review*, 152, 60-73

—— (1987) *Saints and Scholars*, London and New York: Verso

Eco, U. (1979) *The Role of the Reader: Explorations in the Semiotics of Texts*, London: Hutchinson

—— (1990) *The Limits of Interpretation*, Bloomington and Indianapolis: Indiana University Press

Fish, S. (1980) *Is There a Text in This Class? The Authority of Interpretive Communities*, Cambridge, Mass.: Harvard University Press

—— (1981) 'Why No One's Afraid of Wolfgang Iser' *Diacritics*, 11, Spring, 2-13

Foster, H. (ed.) (1983) *The Anti-Aesthetic: Essays on Postmodern Culture*, Port Townsend, Washington: Bay Press

Foucault, M. (1970) *The Order of Things*, London: Tavistock

—— (1977) 'What Is an Author?' trans. D. R. Bouchard and S. Simon, in D. R. Bouchard (ed.) *Language, Counter-Memory, Practice*, Ithaca, N.Y.: Cornell University Press

—— (1983) *This Is Not a Pipe*, trans. J. Harkness, Berkeley, Los Angeles, London: University of California Press

Fowles, J. (1970) *The French Lieutenant's Woman*, St Albans, Herts.: Panther Books Ltd

—— (1982) *Mantissa*, London: Jonathan Cape

Frow, J. (1991) *What Was Postmodernism?*, Sydney: Local Consumption Publications

Gass, W. H. (1971) *Fiction and the Figures of Life*, Boston: Nonpareil Books

Genette, G. (1980) *Narrative Discourse: An Essay in Method*, trans. J. E. Lewin, Ithaca, N.Y.: Cornell University Press
——(1982) *Figures of Literary Discourse*, trans. A. Sheridan, Oxford: Basil Blackwell
Gissing, G. (1968) *New Grub Street*, Harmondsworth: Penguin
Gombrich, E. H. (1972) *Art and Illusion: A Study in the Psychology of Pictorial Representation*, London: Phaidon Press
Grenville, K. (1988) *Joan Makes History*, St Lucia: University of Queensland Press
Henshaw, M. (1988) *Out of the Line of Fire*, Ringwood, Vic.: Penguin
Hofstadter, D. R. (1980) *Gödel, Escher, Bach: An Eternal Golden Braid*, New York: Vintage Books
Holst Petersen, K. (1991) 'Gambling on Reality: A Reading of Peter Carey's *Oscar and Lucinda*' in G. Capone (ed.) *European Perspectives: Contemporary Essays on Australian Literature*, St Lucia: University of Queensland Press, 107-16
Hume, K. (1984) *Fantasy and Mimesis: Responses to Reality in Western Literature*, New York and London: Methuen
Hutcheon, L. (1984) *Narcissistic Narrative: The Metafictional Paradox*, New York and London: Methuen
——(1985) *A Theory of Parody: The Teachings of Twentieth-Century Art Forms*, London and New York: Methuen
——(1988) *A Poetics of Postmodernism: History, Theory, Fiction*, London: Routledge
——(1989) *The Politics of Postmodernism*, London: Routledge
Iser, W. (1974) *The Implied Reader: Patterns of Communication in Prose Fiction From Bunyan to Beckett*, Baltimore and London: Johns Hopkins University Press
——(1978) *The Act of Reading: A Theory of Aesthetic Response*, Baltimore and London: Johns Hopkins University Press
——(1981) 'Talk Like Whales' *Diacritics*, 11, Fall, 82-7
Jameson, F. (1972) *The Prison-House of Language: A Critical Account of Structuralism and Russian Formalism*, Princeton and London: Princeton University Press
——(1975-76) 'The Ideology of the Text' *Salmagundi*, 31-2, Fall–Winter, 204-46
——(1983) 'Postmodernism and Consumer Society' in Foster (ed.) *The Anti-Aesthetic*, 111-25

Jardine, A. (1985) *Gynesis: Configurations of Woman and Modernity*, Ithaca and London: Cornell University Press

Johnson, B. S. (1964) *Albert Angelo*, London: Constable

Kaplan, E. A. (ed.) (1988) *Postmodernism and Its Discontents: Theories, Practices*, London and New York: Verso

Kearney, R. (1984) *Dialogues with Contemporary Continental Thinkers: The Phenomenological Heritage*, Manchester: Manchester University Press

Lanser, S. S. (1981) *The Narrative Act: Point of View in Prose Fiction*, Princeton, New Jersey: Princeton University Press

Lee, A. (1990) *Realism and Power: Postmodern British Fiction*, London: Routledge

Lodge, D. (1977) 'The Novelist at the Crossroads' in M. Bradbury (ed.) *The Novel Today*, London: Fontana/Collins, 84-110

—— (1980) *How Far Can You Go?*, London: Secker & Warburg

—— (1984) *Small World*, London: Secker & Warburg

Lyotard, J.-F. (1984) *The Postmodern Condition: A Report on Knowledge*, trans. G. Bennington and B. Massumi, Minneapolis: University of Minnesota Press

McCaffery, L. (1982) *The Metafictional Muse: The Works of Robert Coover, Donald Barthelme, and William H.Gass*, Pittsburgh, Pa.: University of Pittsburgh Press

McHale, B. (1987) *Postmodern fiction*, New York and London: Methuen

Maclean, M. (1988) *Narrative as Performance: The Baudelairean Experiment*, London and New York: Routledge

Martin, W. (1986) *Recent Theories of Narrative*, Ithaca and London: Cornell University Press

Miller, J. H. (1982) *Fiction and Repetition: Seven English Novels*, Oxford: Basil Blackwell

Murnane, G. (1988) *Inland*, Sydney: Picador

Newman, C. (1985) *The Postmodern Aura: The Act of Fiction in an Age of Inflation*, Evanston: Northwestern University Press

Norris, C. (1987) *Derrida*, London: Fontana

Pirandello, L. (1980) *Six Characters in Search of an Author*, trans. F. May, London: Heinemann

Polan, D. (1988) 'Postmodernism and Cultural Analysis Today' in Kaplan (ed.) *Postmodernism and Its Discontents*, 45-58

Pratt, M. L. (1977) *Toward a Speech Act Theory of Literary Discourse*, Bloomington and London: Indiana University Press

Ricardou, J. (1975) 'La Population des miroirs' *Poétique* 22, 196-226

Robbe-Grillet, A. (1965) *For a New Novel: Essays on Fiction*, trans. R. Howard, New York: Grove Press, Inc.

—— (1968) *Snapshots*, trans. B. Morrissette, New York: Grove Press, Inc.

Rose, M. A. (1979) *Parody/Metafiction: An Analysis of Parody as a Critical Mirror to the Writing and Reception of Fiction*, London: Croom Helm

Ross, A. (ed.) (1988) *Universal Abandon? The Politics of Postmodernism*, Minneapolis: University of Minnesota Press

Said, E. W. (1983) 'Opponents, Audiences, Constituencies and Community' in Foster (ed.) *The Anti-Aesthetic*, 135-59

Scholes, R. (1975) *Structural Fabulation: An Essay on Fiction of the Future*, Notre Dame: University of Notre Dame Press

—— (1979) *Fabulation and Metafiction*, Urbana, Chicago and London: University of Illinois Press

Siegle, R. (1986) *The Politics of Reflexivity*, Baltimore and London: Johns Hopkins University Press

Skei, H. H. (1987) 'Metafiksjon: en grenseoppgang og noen norske eksempler' *Vinduet*, 1, 12-19

Sterne, L. (1967) *The Life and Opinions of Tristram Shandy*, Harmondsworth: Penguin

Thiher, A. (1984) *Words in Reflection: Modern Language Theory and Postmodern Fiction*, Chicago and London: University of Chicago Press

Todorov, T. (1967) *Littérature et signification*, Paris: Larousse

Valenzuela, L. (1987) *The Lizard's Tail*, trans. G. Rabassa, London: Serpent's Tail

Waugh, P. (1984) *Metafiction: The Theory and Practice of Self-Conscious Fiction*, London and New York: Methuen

—— (1989) *Feminine Fictions: Revisiting the Postmodern*, London and New York: Routledge

White, H. (1984) 'The Question of Narrative in Contemporary Historical Theory' *History and Theory* 23 (1), 1-33

Winnett, S. (1990) 'Coming Unstrung: Women, Men, Narrative and Principles of Pleasure' *PMLA*, 105 (3), 505-18

Winterson, J. (1987) *The Passion*, Harmondsworth: Penguin

—— (1989) *Sexing the Cherry*, London: Vintage

Woolf, V. (1966) 'Mr Bennett and Mrs Brown' in *Collected Essays*, vol. 1, London: Chatto & Windus, 319-37

—— (1975) 'Modern Fiction' in *The Common Reader: First Series*, London: Hogarth Press, 184-95

Woolgar, S. (1988) *Science: The Very Idea*, Chichester, London and New York: Ellis Horwood Limited and Tavistock Publications

Zavarzadeh, M. (1976) *The Mythopoeic Reality: The Postwar American Nonfiction Novel*, Urbana: University of Illinois Press

Index

670

If on a winter's night
            evening
Mark Henshaws
John Barthes
            Lost in the
                    funhouse

Roland Barthes by Roland
    Barthes